There's an
Enemy Sub in
Potter's Pond

There's an Enemy Sub in Potter's Pond

George D. Durrant
Matthew B. Durrant

Bookcraft
Salt Lake City, Utah

Library of Congress Catalog Card Number: 81-69931
ISBN 0-88494-439-5

2nd Printing, 1982

Lithographed in the United States of America
PUBLISHERS PRESS
Salt Lake City, Utah

Contents

1

The Maniac

I reckon goin' to Saratoga swimming resort is better than goin' to heaven, on account of you got to die to get to heaven, but you only have to take the bus to get to Saratoga. Our class did it every year — go to Saratoga, that is. Sam had got to the bus early like we said we was going to. He shouted from near the back, "Jake, I got you a seat saved here by the window."

As I was making my way to the back of the bus, I seen E.J. sitting in the back seat two seats behind Sam. "You don't want to sit by Sam, do you, Jake? Sitting by that runt would be worser'n sitting by a girl."

He said it loud, and most everybody on the bus laughed. It weren't that it was particular funny or that everybody wanted to make fun of Sam, it was just that E.J. had said it. I looked away from Sam as I walked by him to sit by E.J. I felt bad about Sam, but I have to admit I was powerful proud E.J. wanted me to sit by him. Nerk come back and sat by Sam, but that didn't help things much. Nerk weren't a whole lot better company than a empty seat.

About half-way to Shepherdsville, as I leaned forward to try and catch Sam's attention, I seen Sarah Easten sitting about five rows up. E.J. seen me looking at her. "Hey, Sarah!" he shouted as loud as a circus caller, "I ought to trade places with you, so you can come back here and sit by Jake."

I ain't never been so embarrassed. I could feel my face reddenin' up as I ducked behind Sam's seat. "Be quiet, E.J.!" I kind of shouted in a whisper.

That only made E.J. want to say more. He was awful fond of kicking a feller when he was down. "Remember when you and Jake danced together in last year's spring festival at the PTA program? Jake ain't talked about nothin' else since."

That was a lie. I'd have told Hitler hisself I liked Sarah before I'd have told E.J. He weren't the kind of feller to tell your deepest secrets to. I wouldn't have cared so much about the whole thing, except for Sarah was awful perty for a girl, and I liked her more than I liked strawberry ice cream on the Fourth of July or watermelon on Labor Day.

Finally E.J. shut up, on account of all Sarah would do was scrunch up her face and look at him like he was some kind of rodent or field rat or something. Problem was, she was probably thinking I weren't a whole lot better. It was awful hard to figure at times whether I'd be better off with E.J. for a friend or a enemy.

As we got in to downtown Shepherdsville, E.J., who was looking out the window, jostled me hard enough to wake a dead man and said, awful serious, "Sit up! It's Rip Snorgan."

He didn't have to say no more. It was the first time I ever seen Rip Snorgan. He was just getting on his bike with a box of Cracker Jacks in his hand and was wearing a dingy T-shirt and old Levi's. I'd heard a slew of stories about Rip Snorgan. Folks said he was a certified maniac, that the only reason he weren't locked up was the nut house wouldn't have him. I knowed nut houses usually weren't too particular, but it weren't no surprise that they made a exception in Rip's case. Folks said he was always catching dogs and cats and skinning 'em while they was still alive, which ain't a particular pleasant hobby. I didn't much want to talk about him, but E.J. seemed bent on it.

"I seen him once before," he said. "He was in a stream by the high school with his pant legs rolled up spearing bullheads. He had a nail he'd sharpened sharper than a needle on the end of a broomstick. He got a fish every time he tried. He'd hold the pole up and laugh as he watched the fish wiggle."

I reckoned it weren't no use trying to avoid the subject, so I says, "You don't reckon he'd ever use the broomstick outside the stream, do you?"

"You mean for killing somebody?" asked E.J. "I don't reckon it'd bother him more'n spittin' in the road. He moved here from Steelville, and killin' there is about as common as chicken farming is here. But Rip Snorgan, they say he was even too ornery for Steelville. I reckon if you did him wrong he'd do you in first and ask questions later."

I was glad Rip was in Shepherdsville and not Saratoga. I reckoned a feller was a lot better off seeing him from a moving bus than up close. I'd never met no maniac, and I weren't exactly hankering to.

By and by we went over the narrow bridge that crossed the Malone River. That bridge always made me nervous as a turtle on a horse track. It looked like it couldn't hold *itself* up, let alone a bus. But it held, and three minutes later we was in my favorite place in all the world — Saratoga.

As soon as the bus stopped, E.J. was out of his seat pushing and shoving to be the first one out. He went straight to the big dressing room, and quicker'n you could spit we had our swimming suits on and was heading for the big indoor pool. I could see the blue water ahead and could smell that swimming pool smell.

Since I weren't the best swimmer in town, I stayed right by the edge of the pool so I could hold on to the side. Besides, I weren't sure how long you had to wait after eating to not get a cramp. Just the same, I went right past the big rope to the deep end. Nobody was going to call me chicken.

I was holding on to the edge in the ten-foot area when, before I knowed it, somebody swum under my legs and popped up next to me. It was Rip Snorgan in the flesh. I about lost my breakfast. He smiled a smile worse than any frown I ever seen and said, "You're that little Denning kid, ain't you?"

I didn't say nothing, on account of my throat was froze. I'll bet Amellia Airhart weren't that skeert when her plane went down in the ocean. I tried going hand over hand on the edge of the pool to get away, but he put his hairy arms on each side of me and grabbed the deck. My heart was jumping like a trapped rabbit. He put his face right up to mine and stared for about a ternity until I looked away. Then he laughed and said, "You got a brother named John, don't you?"

I didn't answer, only croaked, "Please let me go."

"You ain't going nowhere, shrimp. Your brother caused me a whole heap of trouble once and you're gonna pay for it." With that he pried my fingers from the edge and with his arm around my neck hauled me into the deep water.

When we got to the middle, he let me go and whispered, "Swim or die." Then he pushed me down. I was partial to the first choice, but as I was twisting and turning I didn't even know which way was up. Finally, my feet touched the cement bottom. I pushed against it and soon my head popped out of the water. As I started to gasp for breath, he put his giant hand on my head and pushed me down again. Instead of gasping air, all I got was water. It felt like both my lungs was full of water. I couldn't breathe, I couldn't shout. I couldn't see.

The next thing I knowed I was laying on the deck and Mr. Perlman, our bus driver, was kneeling over me. "You all right, Jake?" he asked. "Sam told me what was happening and I hurried as fast as I could."

After Mr. Perlman seen I was okay, he started yelling at Rip, "You must be crazy or something, trying to drown a little kid."

Rip grinned and said back at him, real calm, "I weren't trying to drown nobody. I seen him struggling out in the deep water and tried to save him, except he kept beating me away." Then he turned to E.J. and said, "You seen it, kid. Was I trying to drown him?"

E.J. didn't say nothing at first — just looked down and rubbed the pool deck with the ball of his foot. I could tell he was awful skeert. Then Rip says, all perturbed, "You deaf, kid?"

E.J. said in what was almost a whisper, "Looked to me like he was trying to help Jake and—"

Before E.J. could say any more, Sam shouted, "He's lying. He was trying to drown him—kept pushing his head under water."

Rip turned and glared at Sam. "Why, you little weasel! You and Denning will both pay for this. I wouldn't sleep too easy nights if I was you." I believe he'd have done us in right there, but Mr. Perlman, who lucky for me and Sam was built like about three bull elephants, grabbed him and carted him off to the main office. As he took him, he was shouting that Rip would never set foot in Saratoga again.

I didn't feel much like swimming after that, so I got dressed and went and waited on the bus. I guess Sam seen me, because perty soon he was in the bus, too. "Thanks, Sam," I says.

"You're welcome."

We didn't say nothing more, then nor on the way home. E.J. weren't exactly talkative, neither. He looked like he felt even worser than me and Sam. The girls was all up front huddled around Sarah's seat and talking excited. Every now and again Sarah would turn around and give E.J. a know-it-all smile. I'll bet E.J. woulda liked to cream her.

That night I asked my brother, John, if he knew Rip Snorgan. He laughed and said he did. When I told him what happened, he got madder than I ever seen him before. He told me he caught Rip stealing some coats at school and was dragging him to the principal's office, but let him go when Rip promised never to do it again. Rip was powerful mad, on account of everybody in school was skeert of him except for John.

After a bit, John calmed down some. He put his hand on my shoulder and says, "Don't be afraid of him, Jake. I'm gonna pay him a little visit and see that he never bothers you again."

Still, the only time I weren't skeert at nights was when I knowed John was home. I didn't tell John I was still skeert, on account of I didn't want him thinking I was chicken. When I told Ma, she just said to say my prayers. That helped some, but not enough. I didn't tell Pa, on account of I knowed that being as he was the bravest man in the world he'd never understand. Besides, me and him didn't talk about much of anything.

I'd check in my closet and under my bed every night with a baseball bat. I figured it was just one of them things a feller has to live with. If I didn't have John for a brother I reckon I wouldn't never have slept a wink.

2

The Snake

It ain't easy making your way through a Amazon jungle. Well, I guess I best be honest with you about it—the creek bed really ain't no Amazon jungle, but it's sure as shooting the closest thing to one in Higgins County. E.J. says the creek bed's sticker bushes might be as dangerous as them in some of the two-bit African jungles, but of course nothing like you'd find in a respectable jungle like the Amazon. I reckon E.J. knowed more about Africa than anybody outside of the place, on account of his ma had a perscription to *National Geographic*. She never read it, just liked to plop it out there on the coffee table for show, but E.J., he studied every picture real close.

Nerk was walking up ahead of me, and before I knowed what he was up to I got smacked full in the face with a skinny tree branch. I didn't think it was particular funny, so I says, "Nerk, you try somethin' like that again and you'll wish you was never born."

"I didn't do it on purpose, Jake," he whined back at me. Nerk was the kind of feller that would lie to his own grandma for a plug nickel.

E.J., who was up leading the way, turned and hollered back at me, Nerk and Sam, "If you guys don't keep a lid on it, we ain't gonna catch nothin'."

Fact is, I weren't too anxious to catch nothing anyways. I didn't see how our slingshots would be worth a bucket of beans if we run up against a elephant or a rhinoceros or one of them other dangerous critters E.J. always said we was on the trail of. Lucky thing we hadn't never seen an elephant in the creek bed, let alone capture one. E.J. always said it was me or Nerk's or Sam's fault.

We was about to the clearing. I suppose I knowed the creek bed better than any feller alive, on account of it was my favorite place and only about a mile from our property. When we reached the clearing, E.J. shouted, "We best keep on moving, men. We're sittin' ducks out in the open like this. Them confounded savages got more poison darts than Sally Buford's got freckles."

That's another thing I always thought was a bit peculiar. E.J. was always saying there's a couple million savages that lived in the creek bed, but I ain't never seen a one of 'em. E.J. explained it was on account of what you call "camelflage," but I never seen no camels neither.

I was powerful hungry, so I told E.J. that while I weren't exactly partial to poison darts, I weren't particular excited about starving to death neither, and I'd just as soon we sat down in the clearing and et our peanut butter sandwiches. Sam plops down beside me, pulls out his canteen, and says, "I want to eat, too."

E.J. didn't take too kindly to that. "You two ain't got a thimble-ful of brains between you," he says. "Why, them Pogo Pogo savages would just as soon boil you in hot elephant oil as look at you."

It was a bit cold out, so I says, "Heck E.J., I reckon hot elephant oil would feel downright pleasant on a day like this."

Sam, he laughed on account of he knows a good joke when he hears one, but E.J. only grabbed my arm and started twisting it. "What did you call me?" he says.

"Ouch! I give," I says. "Let me go!"

But he only twisted harder and asked, "What's my name?"

Then I realized what he was after. "Frank Buck," I says.

"Dern tootin'," he says, "and don't you forget it." Then he let me go.

I looked over at Sam and could tell he was considerable put off that I give in to E.J. But just what was I supposed to do? I weren't too anxious to walk around the rest of my life with a crooked arm. I ain't never seen no star basketball player with a arm twisted like a corkscrew.

E.J. was the type that always had to be in charge of things, always had to be the hero. It rankled me at times, but I reckon he was best at it. Seemed like he never did run out of ideas. After we seen "Tarzan, King of the Apes" down at the Corral Showhouse, for the next two weeks E.J. was Tarzan, and me, Nerk, and Sam was the apes. Then, after we saw "Buccaneers of the High Seas," E.J. got to be Captain Peg-Leg and the rest of us was deckhands. And now, after we seen a movie last Saturday about Frank Buck capturing wild animals in Africa and bringing 'em back alive, E.J. was Frank Buck and we was his loyal native helpers.

When we was walking out of the Corral after the show, I said I had a hankering to be Frank Buck, but E.J. said I couldn't. I'd just about had it with doing all the following and none of the leading, so I said, "Then I ain't gonna play."

Sam said, "Me neither. If Jake ain't Frank Buck, I ain't playing."

E.J. didn't say nothing at first, just stomped down on the middle of a condensed milk can so it'd stick on his heel and clank when he walked. After he got it stuck on good, he says, "O.K., Jake. You be Frank Buck and we'll see just how fun it is. What we gonna do first?"

He caught me by surprise, and derned if I could think of one thing to do.

Nerk broke out laughing and said, "Jake, you ain't got the brains to bring a worm back alive, let alone a man-eatin' heyeena. It ain't gonna be a lick of fun unless E.J. is Frank Buck."

It felt downright terrible to be so dumb, and I guess my face showed it.

"It's all right, Jake," says Sam. "Even Frank Buck don't always got to be doing somethin' exciting. He's got scads of regular old everyday things to do, just like everybody else."

E.J. throwed his arms out, all perturbed. "If all we're gonna be doing is a bunch of regular things," he said, "ain't no sense in anybody being Frank Buck. We might all just as well be ourselves, and that'd be about as fun as slopping pigs."

Well, I couldn't think of no way under heaven to argue with that, so I says, "I don't feel much like being Frank Buck today, anyways."

Almost before I could finish my sentence, E.J. says, "Men, we're short one alligator and three zebras. If we aim to get 'em by sundown and bring 'em back alive, we best commence huntin'."

I wanted to kick myself for not thinking of something like that to say when I was Frank Buck, but it was too late now. I'd lost my chance. Sam looked at me all disgusted, so I looked right back at him like it weren't no matter to me. But fact was it did matter. It mattered a whole lot.

Anyhow, that's how we ended up in the creek bed trying to chase down wild and dangerous animals. After E.J. finished twisting my arm, he said the Pogo Pogo savages was most likely eating their lunch, so it probably wouldn't do no harm if we et ours. So as it turned out I got my arm about snapped off for nothing.

We sat down under a willow tree and I commenced to pull a sticker out of my foot as I et my sandwich. Sam looked at me and says, "Jake, if you don't got the toughest feet in all of Rooster Creek, I don't know who has. Here it is November and you're still goin' barefoot."

Well, I have to admit it was downright remarkable. Even though this was the warmest November in years, it was still cold out.

E.J. was a touch rankled, and he says, "My feet are a good sight tougher than Jake's. It's just that my ma won't let me go barefoot because she's afraid my feet would scratch up the living room furniture."

"That's the most ridiculous thing I ever heard," says Sam. "A rhinoceros don't got feet that tough. You wear shoes because your feet would get cold if you didn't and because you're afraid of stickers. You always gotta be the best at everything, but this time you ain't. Jake's feet are tougher than yours, and you know it."

I was partial to Sam's side of the argument, but my arm was still aching, so I didn't say nothing about the matter. Matter of fact, so as to get off the subject, I put my ear to the ground and shouted, "I can hear a whole herd of elephants stampedin' this way. By the sound of 'em, I reckon there must be easy five million of 'em."

To tell the truth, I really didn't hear nothing, but I was afraid if we kept talking about feet Sam was gonna get E.J. mad at me again. And I thought the five million elephants was a right nice idea. I only wish I coulda thought of it when I was Frank Buck. It's a good bit easier to think of ideas about leading when you ain't the leader.

"Hurry up, men." E.J. shouted. "If we don't get out of here them elephants will squash us like a egg dropped off the Empire State Building."

I ripped my shirt a bit climbing over the barbed wire fence, but I didn't reckon my ma would mind much, being as it weren't my Sunday shirt. I went to jump over the irrigation ditch that ran alongside the fence, but just then I looked down and there in the grass was a snake about six inches from my right foot.

I jumped all right — jumped far enough to clear a hundred irrigation ditches. As I sailed through the air, I hollered, "Snake!"

E.J. spun around so sudden that Nerk, who was just a step behind him, crashed into him. E.J. pushed Nerk to the ground and hurried to the ditch bank where I was standing. As he came he was shouting, "Where is this deadly cobra? Frank Buck is ready. We'll capture it and put it in the zoo. People will come from all over the world to see what Frank Buck brung back alive."

In the commotion the snake had snuck away and was hiding somewhere in the two-foot-high grass. I told E.J. it looked more like a regular old water snake than a deadly cobra, but he said there was a whole strain of cobra that was the spittin' image of water snakes. After we looked in the grass for a minute, Nerk says, "There ain't no snake. You made it up."

"Yeah there is. I seen it. It's in here somewhere."

Sam had jumped across the river, and he whispered so that only I could hear, "Say you didn't see it, and let's go."

"No. I seen it," I said back in a loud voice. "I stomped on it with my bare foot. Why, if my feet weren't so tough, I'd be dead of a cobra bite right now." Then I seen it again. It had slithered down into the ditch. "There it is!" I shouted, pointing to the water.

E.J. seen it, and he jumped back away from the water's edge. "Reach in and grab it, Nerk," he yelled.

"You're Frank Buck," says Nerk. "*You* grab it."

I could see that E.J. weren't too happy about being Frank Buck no more, so I says, "I'll be Frank Buck." Since E.J. didn't say nothing against it, I hollered, "It'd take a whole platoon of men to bring a cobra back alive. There ain't but one choice — we best kill it before it kills us."

Well, that weren't no regular thing to do by a long shot, and E.J. and Nerk thought it was a pretty good idea, but Sam says, "It ain't no cobra. It's just a water snake. Ain't no sense in killin' a innocent water snake."

We didn't pay no attention to Sam. By now E.J. had got some of his courage back and was crouching down looking into the creek. I picked up a rock about the size of a football, but it was so heavy it throwed my aim off and I only hit the water by the side of the snake. My rock splashed the snake up out of the ditch, and I'll be derned if the water and the snake didn't hit E.J. full in the face. The snake ended up on his shoulder.

I ain't never seen nobody so skeert. E.J.'s eyes was open so wide they about popped out of his head. He screamed like a coyote and slapped the snake off his shoulder. Nerk was laughing so hard he couldn't breathe. I was afraid to laugh, on account of I knowed what E.J. would do to me, but I was sure laughing hard inside.

I guess E.J. was too embarrassed to be mad at me or Nerk. He pulled out his slingshot and shouted, "That cobra has breathed its last."

We started firing so fast you'd have thought we had machine guns instead of slingshots — all of us except Sam. He was sitting down on the other side of the ditch, leaning against the fence.

I was the first to hit the snake. My rock caught him about two inches behind his head and cut deep into his back, but he just kept right on wiggling. E.J. and Nerk kept firing at him. By and by he slowed down and it got easier to hit him. Finally, E.J. and Nerk put their slingshots back in their pockets. The snake was still moving a little, just enough to tell he was still alive. Blood had turned his silver body red. We sat down and watched him die.

We hadn't noticed it in the excitement, but Sam had clumb back over the fence and was walking home. I jumped over the ditch, ran up to the fence, and shouted after him, "Where ya goin', Sam?"

He stopped and turned around. "Some Frank Buck you are, Jake. You couldn't even bring a helpless little water snake back alive."

By this time E.J. and Nerk had jumped across the ditch and was standing by me at the fence. E.J. shouted out, "Sam, you're just jealous because you was too chicken to help."

"Yeah," Nerk says. "You afraid a little snake would bite you or something?"

I had a empty feeling inside, so I didn't say nothing.

Then E.J. says, "Ah, let him go home. He always ruins everything. Frank Buck ain't got no room in his outfit for a chicken. Nerk, Jake, come on. I seen a zebra a while back when we was walkin' by the canal."

"I ain't going to the canal," I says.

"Why not?" E.J. asked. "Do you want to go home with chicken Sam?"

I was gonna say, "Yeah, I do, and what of it?" but instead I says, "It's pert near four o'clock and I gotta get home to gather eggs." E.J. and Nerk knowed I had to do the eggs every day, so they took off walking toward the canal.

By this time Sam was way ahead of me. I ran until I caught up with him. We walked side by side for a while without either of us saying nothing. Finally I says, "Do you think we oughta go back and bury him?"

"Nah. It don't matter."

We didn't say nothing more until we reached the Alpine Road. Then I says, "I don't feel particular good about what I did."

"Well, then why'd you do it, Jake?"

"I hate snakes. Besides, they ain't worth not killing."

"Says who?"

"Says me."

"No, Jake, that ain't what you say. You ain't listening to yourself."

That was the most ridiculous thing I ever heard. I done my best to apologize, but now I was more than a little peeved, so I says, "You're just jealous on account of I got to be Frank Buck."

Sam didn't say nothing back, just turned down Willow Road and walked away.

I hurried down to the cellar and got the wire egg baskets. In my mind I kept seeing the broken body of the little snake.

3

The Fish

I like watching Ma make bread dough. She reaches down into that big pan of hers, lifts the dough up, squeezes it firmly, and plops it down again. By and by she says, "It's ready to raise." It's yeast that makes it raise, but I couldn't for the life of me tell you how it works. One day I gulped down a spoonful, on account of I thought it might make me raise. I didn't grow none, but I did throw up.

As soon as the dough raises enough, one of three mighty wonderful things happens to it. The best thing is for Ma to roll it out flat, cut it into little pieces, and plop it into some grease for frying. There ain't nothing in the world that tastes as good as a hot scone with butter dripping from it, or maybe with a little honey or peanut butter spread on it.

Other times Ma makes little balls out of it, puts 'em on a greased pan, and bakes 'em in the Monarch oven. The oven has to be just the right heat, but Ma knows exactly how much coal it takes. By and by, she touches her finger to her tongue and then puts it right on top of the stove. It sort of sizzles and she says, "It's just right." I never did dare do that for fear I'd end up with a fried finger. I reckon Ma is right brave as far as mas go. Them white balls brown up into biscuits that would make your tongue quiver, and the smell of 'em goes from the house clear to the other side of Ashley's fox farm. Ma usually takes 'em out of the oven right at supper time. Even when we eat 'em with potatoes and gravy, corn on the cob, and spare ribs, the best part of the meal is always the biscuits.

If Ma don't make scones or biscuits with the dough, she shapes it into little footballs and we have homemade bread for pert near a week. She always tells us to cut off slices with a knife, but I'm partial to digging it out with my hand. That way is a good mite quicker, and besides, I don't care too much for the crust. Ma says eating crust will make my hair curly, but I'm partial to straight hair anyways. Ma always gets mad, but I tell her that her bread is so good I couldn't wait to get at it, and that always cools her down in a hurry.

Just about every time Ma makes bread, she makes two extra loaves for Sam's ma, on account of Sam's ma is sick — got what you call cancer. She goes down and sees Sam's ma every week and takes her bread and other things. Sam's ma can't speak English hardly at all, but Ma and her talk anyways.

It was Friday. I'd just gathered the four o'clock eggs. The chickens couldn't tell time but Pa could, and if I didn't get the eggs gathered on time I'd catch all kinds of heck. I was listening to "Hop Harrigan" on the radio, waiting for my favorite show, "Jack Armstrong," to come on. Ma was peeling potatoes. She was like lightning on them potatoes — she could peel close to five a minute, and usually the peels would hang down a good two feet. She looked over at the dough she'd made about an hour before, then looked at me and said, "Jake, you're such a good boy. How'd you like to do me a favor?"

"Sure, Ma. What?"

"I'll roll some dough up into biscuits and you can carry them down to Sam's mother. Then she can bake them up herself and they'll have hot biscuits for supper."

Well, I weren't too happy about missing my favorite program, and besides, I was still more than a little rankled about what had happened with Sam and the snake. I felt awful bad about killing the snake, but I still didn't think much of the way Sam had acted.

"I'll take 'em up right after Jack Armstrong," I said.

She put her hands on her hips, which was always a bad sign. "Now, Jake, I don't think it will hurt you to miss your program just once."

I knowed it wouldn't be no use explaining to my ma how important listening to Jack Armstrong was, when her mind was set. I'd seen her miss her favorite program, "Ma Perkins," to go to a church meeting. Course, Ma Perkins weren't hardly Jack Armstrong as far as excitement went. She made up the biscuits and I hurried out of the house with a pie-tin full covered with a white dish towel in each hand. When Ma said "good-bye," I didn't say nothing back to her. I knowed that would make her feel perty badly, but I was feeling perty bad myself. I couldn't hurry as fast as I wanted to, on account of I couldn't swing my arms.

I went down the Alpine Road for a block, and at Pardune's I left the tar road and walked a block over to the old Star Flour Mill. Then I turned right and went in the north end of the winding mill lane. If I'd have got the Jack Armstrong walkometer I'd sent for a couple of months before, I'd tell you just how long the mill lane was. But since I sent my Wheaties box tops in late and missed out, your guess is as good as mine. After I come out of the mill lane, it was about a stone's throw to Sam's house.

We didn't play at Sam's place much; he always come up to our farm. I guess it was on account of his ma was sick; and besides, he didn't have a barn, nor a cellar, nor a well, nor a granary, nor nothing fun, for that matter.

I walked up the three stairs and knocked. I could hear the radio playing through the door. "Jack Armstrong, Jack Armstrong, Jack Armstrong." The announcer said it louder each time. Then he'd shout, "The All-American Boy." I'd get goose bumps every time I heard that. I liked Jack Armstrong better than Frank Buck, Tarzan, and Buck Rogers all throwed in together.

I was hoping Sam would answer, but even if he did I weren't sure he'd ask me in to listen. I never seen Sam as upset as when we killed that snake.

Mrs. Tanaka come to the door. She was just a little bit of a woman, with coal-black hair. She looked sick, but she was awful perty for a ma just the same. I ain't saying my ma ain't perty. It's just that she looked like a ma a lot more than Mrs. Tanaka looked like a ma. She smiled, and I could tell she was happy about the biscuits. She said something that I reckon was supposed to be English, but I couldn't make hide nor hair of it. Most times I could understand her a little, but this weren't one of those times. I just smiled back at her and said, "Yes, ma'am." Then I walked down the three cement steps and headed back toward the mill lane.

I knowed that even if I was Jesse Owens hisself I'd never get home in time to hear what happened to Jack and Billy and Betty that day, so I took my time. It had rained earlier in the day and was probably a bit cool for most folks, but just how I liked it.

The trees by the mill lane arched all the way over the narrow road, and the brown and gold leaves touched in the middle. Rooster Creek flowed into and out of Potter's Pond and then came winding down to the mill lane. It ran across the rocks and made a gurgling sound that reminded me of being up Marley's Canyon sleeping in a tent. We'd always pitch right next to a stream. There ain't nothing that can put me to sleep as fast as running water, not even the ten o'clock news on the radio. I never was sure whether it was our town that was named after the creek or the creek after our town, but whichever it was, they was both named Rooster Creek. I guess it was on account of we was the poultry capital of the county. There was really a lot more chickens than roosters, but Chicken Creek ain't got quite the ring Rooster Creek does.

I walked along close to the water checking for muskrats, but didn't see none. Most of 'em stayed closer to Potter's Pond. I didn't blame 'em, on account of I loved to be near that pond myself, it was always so peaceful there. I heard a dove and looked up at a dry branch sticking out above the leaves. I could see him perfect. If I woulda had a B.B. gun I could've dropped him in a second, but to be honest about it I was kind of glad I didn't.

By and by, I got to the place where the creek went in the tunnel and crossed under the road. I sat down, put my toes over the edge of the big cement pipe that'd been put in by the WPA workers a few years back, and stayed there for a while looking at the water. The fast parts of it was white as snow, but the calmer parts close to the banks was almost black.

Then I seen him. My friend the fish. I first seen him back when I was nothing but a little kid. I reckon I was the only feller alive that knowed that fish was there. His head was facing into the current and his tail was lazyin' back and forth like a flag waving in a breeze.

"Hey, fish," I says. "How're things going with you? Boy, if I could go swimmin' every day instead of going to school . . ."

"Who you talking to, Jake?"

I about fell in. At first I thought it was E.J., and I'll tell you one thing, I'd have never heard the end of it if it had been—he never missed a chance to rub in the dumb things you'd done, even if it's been a hundred years since you done 'em—but when I turned around there was ol' Sam grinning at me.

"I weren't saying nothin'," I says.

Sam come up beside me and got on his hands and knees. "Sure you was. I heard you say somethin' about swimming every day." He stuck his head over the edge of the pipe and hollered, "Who's down there?"

I didn't say nothing. Sam just knelt there with his head hanging out over the creek. "Wow!" he says, "it's a beauty."

"It's been here for years." I weren't feeling so dumb anymore. "I'm the only one that knows about it. Well, up until now, that is."

I didn't feel at all bad Sam had found out about the fish. I knowed he'd never tell nobody, and I felt like if anybody'd understand, he would. About that time a sparrow landed on a rock near the fish, and the fish darted out of sight into the tunnel.

Sam looked at me and said, "You sort of like that fish, huh?"

"Yeah, I do." I knowed Sam wouldn't make fun of me. He weren't the kind to make fun of nobody. We walked up toward the mill.

"What happened on Jack Armstrong?" I asked.

"Don't know. When Ma told me you'd been by, I come looking for you. I thought you'd go up past Greenwoods', and it took me a bit to figure to look for you this way."

"You left Jack Armstrong to come and see me?"

"Sure, you're my best friend. Besides, I like biscuits."

I couldn't believe anyone would walk out on Jack Armstrong if they didn't have to. I reckon Sam was my best friend. Everybody liked him, but he weren't what you'd call popular — like E.J. or somebody. He was always one of the last couple of guys chose for basketball and baseball. Problem was, Sam weren't much bigger than most of the kids two grades behind us, and he weren't much better than the girls at sports, but none of that seemed to bother him too much. Nobody could remember the last time he'd got anything but a hundred percent on a spelling test — but I reckon that did him more harm than good.

We was just about to Alpine Road when Sam says, "Jake, you ain't much like them other guys at school. Anybody else woulda tried to catch that fish long ago, but all you do is talk to it. Most of them other guys are too busy trying to be tough to be anything else."

I weren't sure I liked what Sam was saying. I may not have been as tough as E.J., but I sure weren't no sissy. "You won't tell nobody about me talking to that fish, will you?"

"You know I wouldn't do that, Jake." He was right. I knowed he wouldn't.

"I want to thank you for bringing them biscuits. They made my ma cry."

"Don't she like biscuits?"

"Sure she does. She was cryin' because you made her happy. She loves your ma like a sister, and she said you was a ii ko."

"If she likes my ma so much, what's she doing calling me that?"

"Oh, it don't mean nothin' bad. That's how you say 'good boy' in Japanese."

"Them Japanese sure got a funny way of saying things," I says.

"It ain't funny to them. Matter of fact, it sounds regular as pie to 'em — just like English does to you or me."

"Well, you're Japanese just like your ma and pa, ain't you, Sam?"

"Yup."

"Why don't English sound funny to you?"

"I was born here in America and learned English when I was a baby."

"Even if you was born here, you ain't been here no longer than your ma and pa. How come they talk funny?"

"It's harder to learn English for old people."

"Harder than for a baby?"

"Yup, appears that way."

"Japanese babies must be considerable smarter than American babies. My aunt's got a baby that ain't got a brain in its head. All it ever does is say 'goo goo' and spit up all over everybody. Ain't no way that kid is gonna learn something better than a grown-up."

As far as I could tell, Japanese was the derndest language that was ever invented. It didn't have a single word that made any sense. "Sam," I says, "how do you say 'I'm sorry' in Japanese?"

"Gomen nasai."

"Huh?"

"Go-men nah-sigh."

"Well," I says, "gomen nasai about that water snake."

"Yeah, me too."

I practiced all the way home but still almost forgot it. I could see now why Sam was so blasted smart. It'd take a certified genius to remember all them funny words. When I walked through the door, Ma had some biscuits out for me. They weren't hot no more, but awful good just the same. Ma was over pedaling the Singer sewing machine. I walked up to her and says, "Ma, about the way I was acting earlier — gomen nasai."

She stopped sewing, put her arm around my waist, and told me thank you.

"Thank you?" I says. "How'd you even know I said something good?"

She smiled up at me and says, "Because I know you would never say anything to me that wasn't good."

Then she pulled my head down and gave me a kiss. I was awful old for kissing, and I was sure glad none of my friends was around — especially E.J.

4

The Dark

Our teacher, Mrs. Amber, weren't one to put a good thing off. We commenced making cardboard Halloween pumpkins and skeletons as soon as school started in September, and we was cutting out turkeys and pilgrims before our Halloween candy was all et. And now, we was already cutting and pasting Christmas Santas and reindeers. Well, I weren't the best adder nor the best speller around, but I'll tell you one thing, I could cut and paste with anybody. Sam always said I was the best in the school at it.

Mrs. Amber was up front smiling in a way that I knowed meant we was in for something exciting. I was right. "Boys and girls," she says, "today you're each going to put your name in a box and draw someone else's out. You'll then have a month to choose a gift for the person whose name you drew."

I thought that was a mighty fine idea right off. I figured I could always stand another Christmas present.

Each of us printed our name on a little sheet of paper. I wrote mine with a red pen, printing it as best I could, on account of this was one time I didn't want it read wrong. We put our names in a big box Mrs. Amber had made up that had cardboard Christmas trees stuck on each side. I reckon Christmas just wouldn't be Christmas without cardboard. She shook the box a bit and walked up and down the rows letting everybody pull out a name.

I was powerful excited as I reached in. I pulled out two papers at first, but let one of 'em slip back through my fingers. After Mrs. Amber had moved down the row, I turned it over just enough so I could see the name. Sarah! I wanted to jump up on my desk and do a jig. To be honest about things, I'm usually a good bit more partial to the getting part of Christmas than the giving part, but this was a exception. Like I said before, Sarah was powerful pretty —for a girl, anyways. I don't want you to get the idea that I had much liking for girls—it's just that Sarah weren't no ordinary girl. She had the longest hair I ever seen. I don't think she'd had a single haircut in her life. Her hair'd glitter almost like it was gold, and when the sun from the window would hit it just right it was enough to put your eyes out. And that weren't all. She liked sports as much as any boy in school. One day in the lunch room she told me her pa said John was the finest athlete ever to play for Rooster Creek High.

She talked to me every now and again, but she always did it when I weren't thinking of much worth saying. Some nights I lied awake thinking of all kinds of fancy things to say to her, but them was always the nights before days when she didn't say nothing at all to me.

The last row of kids was pulling out their names now. Sam was laughing and smiling that big grin of his like he was always doing. He reached in and pulled out one of the last names. As he opened it, I could see that the name was written in red pen. I was mighty happy. If I coulda picked one person to get my name, it woulda been Sam. He weren't one to do nothing halfway, and I knowed I could count on one of the best gifts in the class.

If I could have planned out how that drawing went, it wouldn't have been no better than it turned out. At first I kind of figured things went so well on account of I'd been good that year, but after giving it a good think, I knowed there must have been some other reason.

Mrs. Amber said the only rule was you couldn't spend more

than a dime. It would take a lot of thinking, but if a feller put his mind to it there was a lot of good things that could be had for a dime. Like you could get two Guess What's, with two pieces of candy and a prize inside.

When me and Sam was walking home that afternoon, I asked him whose name did he get. He looked away and said, "Oh, just some girl's." I could tell by the way his cheeks stuck out he was grinning.

I knowed he was lying, and I kind of figured he knowed that I knowed. Me and Sam had the derndest way of telling what the other was thinking. We never could keep a secret from each other.

About a week later, me and Sam headed on down to the Corral to see a show called *Gulliver's Travels.* E.J. couldn't go with us, on account of he was grounded for shooting a B.B. through one of his ma's Christmas tree ornaments. Sam was gonna sleep up at my place after the show.

It was six blocks to the Corral. When we walked past the fire station, I told Sam about how John had rode in the big fire engine with the rest of the basketball team when they won the first state championship in the history of Rooster Creek High two years back. John was all-state and the biggest hero in the county. I told Sam how I was waiting at J.C. Penney's to see John come riding in on the fire engine. I was so proud I could have busted.

About halfway through, I remembered that I told Sam that story before, but he acted like he was hearing it for the first time. When I finished he says, "Jake, someday when you come back on a fire engine from winning the state championship, I'll be waiting in front of J.C. Penney's telling everybody around me, 'That's my friend Jake, and he's the best dern basketball player that ever put on sneakers.' "

Sam had a knack for saying just the right thing. I told him that was my dream, and he said he reckoned it was one dream that was sure to come true. I could tell he wanted it to come true almost as much as I did myself. There ain't nothing too unusual about wanting something good to happen to yourself, but Sam seemed to take considerable interest in good things happening to me.

Gulliver's Travels was the derndest show. This big old feller by the name of Gulliver runs into a bunch of what you call Lillipunions and there's no end of trouble for him. It was a good thing that E.J. hadn't come or he woulda been Gulliver for the next month, and me, Nerk, and Sam woulda been a bunch of no-account Lillipunions. Nerk might have been good at it because he looked a bit like one, but I can think of plenty of things I'd rather be.

There weren't no moon out that night. We walked up Alpine Road, which was a perfect hiding place for a maniac. There was lots of bushes along it and most of the street lights was busted out. When we got to Sam's house, he went in to get his pajamas while I waited outside. He was in there longer than I expected. It was awful dark and I was more than a little uneasy. Finally, the door opened and he came out.

"Jake," he says, "my pa says I can't sleep at your place after all. He's afraid it'd be a bother for your ma."

"My ma wouldn't care if I brought a pack of coyotes home to spend the night."

"I know that, Jake, but you know how my pa is when he gets his mind made up. I'll see you tomorrow."

This all might seem like a little thing to you, but you probably ain't never had no maniac after you. If E.J. had come we'd have walked home together, since he lives next door. That was the reason I asked Sam to sleep up at my house in the first place—so I'd have somebody to walk all the way home with. I was plenty skeert, but not enough to admit it to Sam. He turned and said good-bye and started up to his door.

Now, I don't want you to think less of me. It weren't that I was skeert of the dark. It was just that I was afraid of what I couldn't see on account of the dark. And what I was afraid I couldn't see weren't bears nor alligators nor nothing like that—it was Rip Snorgan. I'd be partial to a wild bear over a maniac any day. A feller had a fighting chance with a wild animal, but when was the last time you heard of somebody coming out all right from a scuffle with a maniac? And the only thing worse than a maniac is a maniac you can't see coming—except for maybe a maniac you can't see coming who's got a broomstick with a nail stuck on the end.

Sam turned around on his way to his front door and seen that I was still just standing there. I wanted to say something, but couldn't find it in me. He walked on back to me and says, "Jake, didn't I leave my basketball up at your place? Let me ask my pa if I can run up with you and get it real quick."

Well, I didn't think he left it and I didn't see how it mattered if he did, being as he wouldn't be shooting no baskets before he came up in the morning anyways, but I weren't about to argue with him.

I was still a bit skeert as we walked up the old lane. Rip wouldn't be afraid of attacking the both of us, but at least there was a good chance that one of us would get away to run for help. I'm ashamed to say it, but I was hoping if that happened the one of us who ran for help would be me. Course, that was mostly because I was a faster runner than Sam. Sam kept laughing and telling jokes as we walked along, and that helped considerable.

When we got to my place Sam turned to leave, and I says, "What about your basketball?"

"Oh, well," he says, "I just remembered that I'm coming back tomorrow, anyways. We'll see you, Jake."

Then he turned and walked away. As he went down the road, I stood on the porch and watched him. He had as much reason to be afraid of Rip as me, but if he was skeert, he did a mighty fine job of hiding it. I watched him in the light of the street light until he was all the way down to Halls'. Somehow, I knowed he'd make it home safe.

5

The Attack

The days seemed to get longer the closer it got to Christmas, especially Sundays—which was long anyways. The Christmas of 1941 was just eighteen days away and was shaping up to be my best ever. Right after church and Sunday dinner, Sam come up and we played basketball for a couple of hours in the barn. A few years back John nailed a rim up on the south wall. Well, it weren't a real rim, just the top of one of them ol' wooden barrels Mr. Macon'd bring clabbered milk in to mix with wheat mash for feeding our chickens. The hoop was smaller than the regulation basket we had outside. Matter of fact, it weren't much bigger than our beat-up old leather ball. But that didn't bother me as much as most fellers. I ain't normally one to brag, but I could have made 50 percent through my ma's wedding ring. John said I was about forty times as good as he was when he was my age, and John was one of the best high school basketball players this ol' town ever saw. Some folks, like Sarah's Pa, said he was the best.

We'd play basketball on our outside basket until the snow would come, and then we'd move into the barn for the winter. John always said if a feller aimed to be good at a sport like basketball, he best practice all year round. The more hay Pa fed our Jersey cow, Bessie, the more room we had to play. For about two weeks just before the snow cleared up outside, we'd have the whole barn floor for a court.

Sam used to play basketball with me a lot. Most of the time he'd do the rebounding. None of my other friends was too partial to rebounding, but Sam didn't seem to mind. At least he never complained about it. Like I said before, he weren't too good a player to begin with, so I reckon he was just glad to be able to play at all with somebody as good as me.

I was shooting awful accurate that day even for me. I got way back in the corner and shot up over the rafter — went right through. Didn't even touch the rim. Sam shouted, "Great shot, Jake" and grabbed the ball and throwed it back to me. "You do that again and you're a all-American."

Sam was always saying stuff like that and I didn't mind it a bit. Even if he weren't too good hisself at basketball, he could sure tell when somebody else was. "I can see you on that red fire engine," he hollered.

I shot another from the same spot and derned if I didn't make it again. Now I don't really expect you to believe this — because Sam and me seen it with our own eyes and we didn't hardly believe it ourselves — but I made *seven* in a row! I'm telling the Bible truth. I missed my eighth try, but as far as I know I set a world's record. I never seen anybody, not even the big guys, not even John — I never seen nobody hit more than three in a row over the rafter. I couldn't wait to tell John, on account of I knew how proud he'd be of me. He was always telling his friends that I'd be a sure-fire all-stater when I growed up. About then I told Sam I had to go eat, and he said he best go home, too. He was heading out the south gate of our place when he turned around and says, "See you in school tomorrow."

I didn't appreciate him ruining a time like that by bringing up school. It was like somebody talking about chicken liver after you just finished a bowl of banana pudding. I said good-bye anyways. Before I even had the door shut, Ma says, "Have you been out there without a coat?"

Ma weren't exactly Sherlock Holmes. She had a nasty habit of asking questions that anybody with two eyes in their head wouldn't need to ask. I said I'd wear one next time and ran over to the little washroom just off our kitchen, where John was scrubbing up. "John!" I shouted, "guess how many I made in a row over the rafter?"

He set the soap down, turned, and said, all upset, "Basketball don't matter no more. Nothing like that matters no more." I hadn't never seen John that way, nor heard him talk so crazy. Basketball was as important to him as it was to me — and that was perty dern important.

Then Ma says, "You boys be quiet. Your pa is trying to listen to the news."

I looked over at Pa in his overalls and blue plaid shirt, sitting in his rocking chair in the corner of our big kitchen. Pa never did say a whole lot with his mouth, but he could sure say a bundle with his eyes. He never took too kindly to nobody saying nothing when the news was on, and he was glaring at me like I was a chicken poacher. John pulled a chair over closer to our old Atwater Kent radio, and Ma seemed a good bit more interested in listening than usual.

I washed my hands and sat at the table waiting to eat. Ma was frying up some pork chops. The news seemed to go on longer than usual. I heard the newsman say something about Pearl Harbor and bombers, but I didn't really understand the rest. Pa turned off the radio, and nobody said much as we started eating. Finally, John broke the silence by saying, "I ain't waiting to be drafted. I'm joining the marines."

"Oh, John," Ma says, with her eyes all watery like she was aiming to cry. "Don't be in such a hurry. This may not be as serious as it seems."

That made Pa madder than a hornet. "Ain't as serious as it seems?" he yelled. "They blew up every ship in the entire U.S. Navy. This ain't no Sunday School picnic. This is war!"

That's when Ma really started crying, but Pa didn't seem to pay it much attention.

"It won't take but three weeks to blow 'em up," John said, as he reached over and put his hand on Ma's. "It'll be over before you know it. There ain't no need to worry. Japan has made a big mistake starting a war with the U.S. of A."

I was a bit afraid to say anything just then, so I waited until dinner was over and followed John out to milk the cow. When we got to the barn, I says, "John, what's a Pearl Harbor?"

"It ain't a what, it's a where. It's a place out in the Pacific. At least, it used to be in the Pacific. The Japanese blowed it clean off the map. That's why I'm going away to fight 'em."

"What business you got fightin' 'em, John?" I asked.

I could see John didn't think that was a particular good question. "What do you mean, what business do I got fighting 'em? Pearl Harbor is American property, and we are Americans. If we don't do something, they'll do it again."

"If they already blowed it clean off the map, what sense would there be in them doing it again?"

"Of course they wouldn't blow up Pearl Harbor again. They'd pick a place that hadn't been blown up — like Rooster Creek. Do you reckon Rip Snorgan would have stopped bothering you if I hadn't put an end to it right off?"

Well, it weren't no surprise to me that Rip was to blame for Pearl Harbor. I just couldn't figure what he had to do with the war. "I know Rip wouldn't have stopped if you hadn't done something, but them that bombed Pearl Harbor ain't never beat me up," I says.

"That ain't the point. What I'm saying is that if anybody beat you up it would be like they'd beat me up, and I wouldn't let 'em get away with it, because they beat up a Denning and I'm a Denning. If somebody come into town and burned down the Morgans' barn, it'd be like they burned down our barn, because Morgans are Rooster Creekers and we are Rooster Creekers. The U.S. of A. is like a whole bunch of Dennings and a whole bunch of Rooster Creekers jammed all together. If a bunch of enemy planes bomb *some* of us, they best be ready to answer to *all* of us."

Well, all that still didn't explain why the Japanese hated basketball and Rooster Creek so bad, but I could see that John didn't feel like answering no more questions.

I walked out past the cellar to the coal shed, cut some kindling from some old boards, filled up the coal bucket, and with a pile of kindling in one arm and a bucket of coal in the other hand I headed back to the house. I put the coal by the side of the stove and the kindling between the hot water tank and the wall. Then I sat down in Pa's rocker, since Pa was out fixing the door to the granary, and looked out of the big bay window. It was getting dark outside now and the window was all frosted over.

By and by Pa come in, so I jumped out of his chair and went to the table to read the funny paper — the only part of the paper worth reading. I read Nancy, Tarzan, and Little Abner, but they didn't seem as funny nor as exciting as usual.

Pa was listening to the news again. Ma was peeling apples on the other side of the radio from him. She seemed more upset than anybody.

"Why'd they do it, Hank?" she asked, with her voice all aquiver.

Pa looked over at her all disgusted and asked "How should I know? I ain't Hirohito, you know." Ma didn't ask no more questions after that.

Pert near half a foot of snow fell during the night. My bedroom was in the back of our house on the north side. It was nice and cool in the summer, but I sure paid for it in the winter, when it about made a icicle outa me. I had enough blankets on my bed to be mistook for Mount Timpanogos.

I jumped out of bed and got dressed as fast as I could. It was either do that or have my feet freeze to the floor. Ma was frying some bacon. Sad to say, but it smelt a good bit better than it tasted. Dad made it powerful salty so as to preserve it, and I didn't have much use for it. It woulda probably been a good idea to send some to the Japanese to pay 'em back for what they did to Pearl Harbor. I rubbed my hands together as I held them over the stove.

Pa had been up for an hour doing the morning chores, and he was just now coming back to the house. John had already milked, and Ma was pouring the fresh milk from the bucket through a cloth into tin pans to be stuck in the ice box. She did that to take out the little pieces of straw and other things that had got in it.

John and Pa washed up and we all sat down to eat. The morning news was on. It was hard to make out just what was going on, but I could tell that it was mighty serious.

John said he was gonna join up that day. Ma begged him to wait, but he wouldn't have none of it. "Ma," he says, "I ain't got much choice. Me and Almie and some of my other friends talked it over and we're going up to Steelville today to join the marines."

Ma didn't cry. I guess she'd about cried herself out last night. Her eyes was red and puffy.

After John and Pa left the kitchen I asked Ma if there was gonna be school.

"Of course there's gonna be school," she says. "Now, why would you ask a question like that?"

"John told me that on account of the war, ain't nothing matters no more — not even basketball."

She said school would always matter. Them Japanese sure had their priorities mixed up. Stopping basketball and at the same time letting school go right on. It sure didn't make no sense to me.

I liked new snow. I'd always pretend I was walking on a bunch of clouds. It was especially fun walking where nobody'd been yet. I stopped to pick up Sam like I always did, but his ma come to the door and only opened it a crack.

"Good morning, Mrs. Tanaka," I says. "Is Sam ready to go?"

She was acting awful strange and didn't seem to want to let me in. "Sam sick," she said. "He no go school today." She shut the door before I could say more.

I could hardly believe what my ears was hearing. For each of the past three years Sam got a certificate for not missing a day of school. I knowed he'd have to be powerful sick to stay home. He was as proud of them certificates as he was of anything he owned. They had his name written all fancy on 'em with a whole slew of squiggly do-da's attached to it.

It weren't nearly as much fun walking the rest of the way to school alone as it woulda been with Sam along. Then, all of a sudden I wished I woulda stayed home too. There was somebody walking toward me about a quarter of a mile down the road. I stopped and almost froze, not so much 'cause I was cold as 'cause I was skeert. It was Rip Snorgan.

I said a prayer inside that he hadn't seen me, and I turned down Birch Street. It took me a block out of my way, but that was a good bit better than getting myself kilt. I'd have gone a hundred miles out of my way if I woulda had to. I couldn't figure out what he was doing up here, being as he lived south of town. He didn't seem to have nothing to do but wander the streets like a stray dog, only going to school when he felt like it, on account of the truant officer was afraid of him.

I turned off Birch down Center Street. I kept looking back, but he didn't come. He must not have recognized me. I crossed the railroad tracks, and then I could see the kids playing Fox and Geese in a big circle they made in the new snow. Both sides wanted me on their team, on account of I was almost as good at Fox and Geese as I was at basketball, and that's perty dern good.

Looked like the teachers was gonna let us play right up to the bell, so I guess the war weren't gonna stop us from playin' Fox and Geese. I come to find out later on that day that Pearl Harbor hadn't changed nothing about spelling nor adding nor history neither. Them Japanese was hard to figure. I couldn't see how anybody in their right mind could be down on basketball but partial to spelling.

6

The Enemy

The bell rang and I ran through the front door of the school. I took the stairs two at a time like I always did. It was against the school rules, but I hadn't never been caught. I hung up my coat and took my seat in the back near the window and looked across the room at Sam's empty desk. We woulda sat next to each other, but the first day of school Mrs. Amber had made us sit in alphabetical order. We was gonna tell her we was brothers and both named Denning, but we was afraid if she found out we lied she'd have had it in for us the whole year and maybe even told our mas.

When she called the roll we all said "present" good and loud, on account of if she ever had to call your name twice for not saying it loud enough the first time she'd scowl at you like you'd kilt her cat. Funny thing was today she was the one that was calling the names too quiet. I almost didn't hear her when she said mine.

When she called Sam's name, there of course weren't nothing but silence. She waited, but nobody said nothing. She looked at

Sam's empty seat and for a few seconds just stared. Then she lowered her head a little and put her hand up to her eyes.

I guess she was as taken back as I was that Sam was missing his first day of school in three years. She seemed to be taking it awful hard, so I yelled out, "He's sick today."

She didn't seem to hear me — at least, she didn't say nothing back at me. She took her hand down from her eyes and finished calling the roll. After she called out Bernie Wooden's name she closed her roll book, walked over to the window, and looked out. We all sat there waiting for her to say something, but she didn't — just kept looking out. She weren't looking at the snow, seemed to be looking way beyond the railroad tracks and even past the mountains. I was feeling awful uneasy. It was as quiet in that room as a chicken coop after sundown.

Finally she turned and walked back to her desk. She opened a drawer, pulled a paper napkin from a box, and touched each eye. Then she says real soft, "Please forgive me, boys and girls, but this is a very hard morning for me." After that she started crying for no reason at all and says, "I love you all so much — so very much."

She was crying real quiet, looking at the back of the room, but not really looking. Then she stood up and started to say, "My son . . ." She didn't finish, just turned and walked real fast out of the door.

By and by the door opened again and our principal, Mr. Larson, come in. He was standing all at attention and real serious. He says, "Boys and girls, our great country is at war. We've never lost a war and we won't lose this one. We must all be patriotic and willing to make sacrifices. Things will not be the same. Many of your brothers and some of your fathers will have to go to war. Some might even be killed, but we will win."

Then he said more softly, "Mrs. Amber's son Kent is in the navy stationed at Pearl Harbor, and she hasn't received word yet on what's become of him. It sure is a crying shame that this all happened."

He finished by telling us to be sure and pray for Mrs. Amber's boy Kent, for all the other soldiers, and especially for President Roosevelt. Then he wrote some arithmetic up on the board for us to figure. They was a lot easier problems than the ones Mrs. Amber always gave us, and even for me they didn't take much thinking. As I was figuring them, I was wondering about Kent Amber. He'd played on the state championship basketball team, and him and John was perty good friends. I wondered if it would do any good to pray if Kent was already dead, but I figured it sure wouldn't hurt none. Ma said that prayers that you think is just about as good as the ones you say out loud, so I said one of the think kind.

It was a long day at school. Mr. Larson kept coming back in to give us more problems. I reckon we did more arithmetic that day than I ever knowed had been invented. The problems was a whole lot harder after Sally Armor told Mr. Larson how easy the first ones was. Sally might have known a lot about arithmetic, but she didn't know nothing about nothing else. Mr. Larson said Mrs. Amber would probably come back tomorrow, but that if she didn't we'd have a substitute. I weren't particular happy to hear that, on account of I never seen a substitute that weren't as mean as a rattler.

Finally the bell rang. I pulled my coat off the hook, zipped it up tight, and walked out into the cold air. The sky was clear now and it was a good mite colder than it had been in the morning.

I decided to stop by and see how Sam was doing. I could tell by the tracks in the snow that nobody'd been in or out of the Tanaka house that day except me. I knocked. Inside, Sam's dog, Arnie, barked. Sam's pa shouted some words I couldn't understand. Then the door opened and there stood Sam.

His eyes was red and it was like there was something different about him. He didn't say "Hi" nor smile nor nothing, just looked down at the porch. "You still feeling sick, Sam?" I asked. He shook his head from side to side, but still didn't say nothing. He was acting awful strange but looked healthy enough.

"Hey, if you're feeling better," I says, "why don't you come out and play for a bit?"

"My ma says I ain't allowed to go nowheres, not even to school."

"Why in blazes not?"

"She says it might not be safe for a while."

"She must have seen Rip Snorgan pass here today," I says.

"No. It ain't Rip. It's everybody."

Before I could ask him what in turnation he was talking about, his ma come to the door and says, "Sam no play." Sam looked down and turned away as his mother closed the door. I'll be derned if I could figure out what was going on.

That night at supper when Ma asked me how I done at school, I told her about Mrs. Amber. I could tell she felt awful bad about it, so to change the subject I told her that Sam'd been sick and missed school for the first time in over three years.

Well, I didn't even think Pa was listening, but he slammed the newspaper down next to his plate and says, "He ain't sick. He's skeert. He's one of 'em."

"One of what?" I says.

"One of the enemy."

I knowed Pa was making a terrible mistake, and even though he was already mad I says, "He ain't no enemy. He's my friend."

"Ain't no difference if he was your friend or your great-uncle. He's one of the enemy now."

I felt strange—kind of like my whole body was a funny bone and I just hit it on the corner of the table.

Ma was powerful mad. "Hank," she says, "there's no reason to talk to a boy like that. The Tanakas are good people. They can't be blamed for what happened thousands of miles away. They're Americans—just like us."

"Americans!" Pa shouted. "Just because they got some piece of paper don't change their being the enemy. No telling when they'll blow up a railroad or something."

I couldn't eat no more. I stood up and began to leave. Pa was still yelling at Ma, so he didn't try to stop me, even though I hadn't finished all my food. I walked out to the barn. A cold wind whistled through the openings where the boards had shrunk some through the years.

I picked up the ol' ball and shot up at the basket that was nearly straight above me. I missed. John was right—basketball didn't seem much fun anymore. I tried again and missed. If Sam had seen me miss them easy shots, he probably would have said something like, "Come on, Jake, you ain't never gonna make all-American shootin' like that."

But what did he know about all-American?

I picked up the ball and without even really thinking threw it at the cow. It hit her on one of her horns and bounced through the manger out into some wet cow manure. As I walked slowly past her, she looked at me like she thought I was crazy, but then again I reckon that's how cows always look at people. I picked up the ball and started rubbing it with dry hay to get it clean.

I remembered when Sam's family first moved in. They come to town to help Giles Draper on his farm. When we asked Sam if he wanted to play golden rod, he smiled and said he did. We drew a big circle in the dirt and told him we'd blindfold him and give him a broom handle to swing at us while we stayed in the circle and tried not to get hit. He smiled and said he didn't want to hit none of us, but we said he could just hit us soft. He laughed as we blindfolded him.

After we made sure he couldn't see, we told him to grab the broom handle. What he didn't know was that we'd put the handle in a big wet pile of cow manure. After he grabbed it, he threw it down and yanked the blindfold off. He looked at his hands and started laughing. Then he chased us around a bit. We done that to a lot of newcomers to town, but none of 'em ever laughed.

I liked ol' Sam from then on. Matter of fact, like I said before, we was best friends. Just the same, I didn't know he'd help the enemy. He never said nothin' about nothin' like that. I wished he never moved to Rooster Creek.

I headed to the coal shed and run into John coming with the milk bucket. I says, "Hi, John," but he looked at me real stern and says, "That's Private Denning. I'm a marine now, and I'll be off to Fort Pendleton in three days."

I couldn't believe it—at least, I sure didn't want to. He sat down on the three-legged stool and started milking the cow. "Why do you got to go, John?" I asked.

"I explained all that to you yesterday."

"You didn't say nothing about going to no fort. I thought forts was for fighting Indians, not Japanese."

"I ain't going to Fort Pendleton to fight nobody, just to learn how to fight 'em."

"You already know how to fight. You ain't afraid of nobody."

"I don't know how to use no machine gun, do I?"

Then I says, "Why can't you fight 'em here?"

John got all disgusted. "For one simple reason," he says. "There ain't no enemy army here. What am I supposed to do, put a ad in the *Tokyo Tribune* that says, 'Any enemy soldiers wanting to fight John Denning should report to Box #17 Willow Street in Rooster Creek, U.S.A.'?"

Well, I could see John had his mind set, so I says, "Then I'm going with you."

"That's crazy," he says. "You ain't big enough to lift a machine gun, let alone fire it. You stay here and do your part at home. There'll be lots of ways you can help."

Without saying no more I turned and walked to the coal shed. I didn't want John to see me cry.

I couldn't sleep that night thinking about John being gone. When John was away on dates, I'd lie in my bed and hear all kinds of suspicious sounds. I never did look out, on account of I was afraid Rip would be looking in. But when I'd hear the door open, I'd know John was home and I'd be asleep before the door shut. Now, the door would never open no more. There was no telling what Rip would do once he found out John was gone. We didn't even have no locks on our doors. The longer I lied in my bed that night, the more I was thinking maybe Sam was the cause of all this, just like Pa said. I decided I'd been wrong in ever being a friend to Sam.

I took the long way to school the next day, on account of I didn't want to even go near Sam's house. I thought for sure he'd stay home again, but when I got settled in my chair at school, I looked across the room and there he was working out some arithmetic problems like nothing had changed.

Even though the bell rang, Mrs. Amber weren't sitting at her desk. We all just sat around talking for fifteen minutes — everyone except for Sam, that is — until finally Mr. Larson come in with some lady I hadn't never seen before, neither of 'em looking too happy.

"Boys and girls," he said, "I have some sad news. Mrs. Amber learned last night that her son Kent was killed when the ship, the U.S.S. *Arizona* was sunk in Pearl Harbor. This here is your substitute teacher, Miss Wrenchler."

Sam lowered his head to his desk. It was then I decided never to say another word to him.

7

The Hole

The next day E.J. said he got a letter from General Douglas MacArthur appointing him a captain in the U.S. Army. He wouldn't let me and Nerk see it on account of it was one of them top secret documents. MacArthur wanted E.J. to round up a platoon of the bravest men he could find to patrol Rooster Creek for enemy troops. When I told E.J. the only Japanese around was Sam's family, he said MacArthur was powerful concerned about the Tanakas and wanted us to keep a sharp eye on 'em.

MacArthur also said in the letter that being as E.J. was one of the bravest fellers in the whole U.S. Army, he could call him Doug if he wanted, but if any of the men in E.J.'s platoon was to call him anything but General MacArthur, they was to be court-marshalled.

E.J. appointed me a corporal and Nerk a admiral. Then he said to Nerk, "Being as a corporal is higher than a admiral, you got to do everything Jake tells you to do. It don't matter if he tells you to go and spit in your ma's eye, you gotta do it."

It sounded like a mighty fine plan to me, but Nerk said if that was the case he didn't want to be in no army.

"It ain't a matter of wantin' or not wantin'," said E.J. "You are what you called 'drafted,' and that means you ain't got no choice."

"Says who?"

"Says me!"

"Well, who says you can say?"

"MacArthur says I can say, you numbskull."

Since Nerk was probably the dumbest fellow ever born, he just kept right on arguing. "Who says MacArthur can say?"

That really got E.J.'s dander up. I could tell he was close to hitting Nerk. "Ain't nobody needs to say nothin' to MacArthur. He's the commander and the chief of the whole U.S. Army, and he can do anything he dern well pleases. There ain't a single rule that's any concern to him. If he wants to eat candy for dinner, he eats. If he wants to stay up past his bedtime, he stays. If he wants to skip church on Sunday, he skips."

"It don't make me no never mind," says Nerk. "I'm going home."

"MacArthur ain't gonna take kindly to this. He just might charge you with desertion."

"What's desertion?" asked Nerk.

"That's most likely the dumbest question ever been asked," says E.J. "I thought everybody knowed what desertion is. Why, even my little sister knows what it is." Then he looked at me and said, "Jake, go on and explain to this knucklehead what desertion means."

I was in a awful mess. I kicked the ground a couple of times. Finally I says, "Why, it's a . . . it's when you don't get no dessert."

E.J. thought a second and says, "That's right. MacArthur'll call your ma and see that you don't get no dessert for a whole year."

Nerk was partial to sweets. He said he'd stay in the army if he didn't have to spit in his ma's eye and if the next recruit who joined up would have to do everything he said. E.J. said that was all right by him, and I promised to never make him spit nowhere, so he said he'd stay.

I had a powerful hankering to tell him some things to do, but since I was afraid he'd get all upset and want to go home again, I held back. I found out it ain't much fun being over somebody if you can't make 'em do whatever you want 'em to do, but at least I didn't have to take no orders from Nerk.

E.J. told me that because I could draw good I was to draw up a map of Rooster Creek to put on the wall of our headquarters. It turned out perty good, and when I showed it to E.J. the next day he said he would promote me from corporal to private first class. I said he didn't have to as long as he didn't promote Nerk. Our headquarters was the old tree house John and his friends built a few years back out behind the barn. We had our top secret meetings there every day. Our password was so secret that even MacArthur didn't know what it was, and I don't reckon I even ought to tell you now.

In our first meeting E.J. said I was to be in charge of scouting Potter's Pond. I was always glad to go to Potter's Pond for any reason, but I didn't see why it needed scouting. E.J. explained it was on account of submarines.

"Jake," he says, "it won't be long before you're gonna see a periscope pop up just out beyond the cattails. And when that happens, just as sure as shootin' there's a enemy sub in Potter's Pond."

"How in turnation are submarines gonna get from the ocean to Potter's Pond?" I asked.

I thought it was a perty good question, but E.J. just looked at me like I was stupid or a girl or something and says, "Ain't you never heard of ground water?"

"Ground water?" I says. "What in turnation's ground water?"

"Your pa got a well don't he, Jake?"

"Sure he's got a well."

"And just where do you think that water comes from?"

That was something I hadn't never thought too much about, so I said I didn't have the slightest.

Then E.J. said, "The water you get from a well is what you call ground water. Anyplace the ocean's got ground over it you got ground water. Boats got to stop when they get to a shore, but submarines can just keep right on going under the shore in the ground water and can end up in any pond they dern well please. And if they end up in Potter's Pond with nobody watching, we'll all be eating with chopsticks before you can say Jack Robinson."

Well, I have to admit I didn't know a lick of that. I guess that's why E.J. was a captain and I was just a corporal. I reckon he was as smart as any of them army generals.

E.J. assigned Nerk to be in charge of standing guard over the Tanaka's house. Nerk weren't too crazy about that and said he'd rather scout Potter's Pond for submarines, but E.J. said that would be much too dangerous for an admiral.

Then Nerk says, "I don't see why we even need anybody guardin' over the Tanaka's house."

"If we don't guard 'em," says E.J., "they might build a submarine out in their barn and carry it out to Potter's Pond."

"Subs are too big to carry," says Nerk.

"Not if you got a tank to tow it, dummy."

I woulda reminded E.J. that the Tanakas didn't have no barn, but I could see that he was perty mad as it was. I kept my mouth shut.

"Seems to me all we is doing is guardin'," says Nerk. "Ain't we gonna do no fightin'?"

I could tell right off that was a stupid question, even for an admiral. "Nerk," I says, "how we gonna fight the enemy army if we got no way to get to where they is? They're all the way across the ocean and we ain't got no boat nor submarine."

I was gonna say more, but E.J., he jumps in and says, "Put a lid on it, Jake. Admiral Cordon's got a perty good idea here. Matter of fact, I know a way we can get to where the enemy army is without a boat or a submarine. From what I understand, if we was to dig a hole straight down, we'd end up in China, and China ain't but a stone's throw from Japan."

"Where'll we start digging?" asked Nerk.

"Let's look at the map Jake drew up," says E.J. After about a minute he says, "Looks to me like if we dig just behind the flour mill we oughta end up in Shanghai."

"I thought we was goin' to China," Nerk says.

E.J. looked at him real disgusted. "Shanghai is in China. Matter of fact, it's the biggest city in the world—got more people than Shepherdsville, South Fork, and Rooster Creek combined."

To be honest about it, I didn't know none of that myself, but I acted as if I did and looked over at Nerk like he was the dumbest feller ever born. Fact is, I don't reckon that was too far from the truth.

We dug some that night, but didn't get down too deep. E.J. said we best be careful to dig straight or else we'd end up in England or Arizona or somewheres. It was cold and awful hard work and I got a couple of blisters on my hands, but then I don't reckon war is supposed to be easy. E.J. said he figured it would take upwards to a month to dig all the way through, and that was if it didn't snow too much. We'd have got down deeper, but I had to go gather eggs.

I was feeling perty proud of how things was going and being a corporal and all until I seen that ornery hen of ours. As far as I could figure, it just weren't right for a corporal to be afraid of no hen. I reached out to grab her by the head, but she cocked, ready to fight. Since I was behind in my work anyways, I left her alone. I meant to go check Potter's Pond for submarines after I finished, but I was too tired. I didn't reckon MacArthur would mind if I missed just one day.

We worked on that confounded hole every night for pert near two weeks. We had to work at night on account of we never knowed when we was gonna break through to China and we wanted to do it when the Chinamen was asleep. It was easy going at first, because being as E.J. was a captain, he'd order me to do the digging, and being as I was a corporal, I'd tell Nerk to dig, and me and E.J. would sit under the big willow tree.

Nerk weren't too partial to that arrangement, and after about a half-hour he said that if we didn't all dig, he was going home. He was a hard one to keep satisfied, wouldn't listen to reason on account of his brain ain't no bigger than a pea, so we all dug— even though E.J. said officers weren't supposed to work side by side with enlisted men.

It was mighty slow going. After two weeks, we weren't but four feet down, and that's stretching it some. E.J. said the dirt would soften up once we got to what you call the core of the earth, and we'd be popping our heads up in China before we knowed it. He said the first thing we'd see in China would be a sign that says Kilroy Was Here. It was a joke, of course, and I laughed, but truth was it wouldn't have surprised me a bit.

I was a bit tired of digging and I still weren't sure it could even be done, so I says, "The core of a apple is a good mite harder than the outside," but E.J. he says, "Is the world a apple, Jake?"

I reckon he had a point there, so I didn't say no more. At least, I didn't say no more that day. By the next day I'd just about had it. I was even wishing MacArthur had never heard of E.J.

Finally I says, "E.J., by the time we make China, the war'll be over."

E.J. didn't take too kindly to that. "If that's the way you're thinkin'," he says, "that's the way it'll turn out. Your problem, Jake, is you ain't got what you call a positive altitude."

"I sure don't," I says, "and I'll collar anybody says I do."

"No, no," says E.J. "Ain't nothin' bad about a positive altitude. Matter of fact, my pa says there ain't nothin' better. He learned about 'em working in a CCC camp a few years back. If you got one of 'em, it means you can do anything you dern well please."

"You mean even if you ain't a general like MacArthur?"

"It don't have nothin' to do with rank, it just has to do with what you're thinkin' inside your head. If we think we can dig through to China, then by golly we can, and there ain't no doubt about it."

"If we can do it just by thinking in our heads," I says, "how come we're digging this here hole with our hands? Why don't we just kick back against this mill and think ourselves all the way to China?"

"It ain't enough just to have a positive altitude, you got to get in and do the work, too."

"Well, if we got to do the work anyways, what good is one of these positive altitudes?"

"Jake, do you use your head for anything besides holding your hair up off your shoulders? Your problem is you ain't never tried it."

He was right. I hadn't. So I says, "Suppose I want to be nine feet tall, could I do that just by thinking it?"

"Just as sure as we're sitting here talking."

"How do I go about it?" I says. I figured being nine feet tall would be powerful handy when it come to basketball.

"Jake," says E.J., "ain't nothing easier. All you gotta do is believe you can do it. Suspectin' don't count for nothin'. You gotta believe it."

I reckoned it was worth a try, so I closed my eyes and commenced believing. I was thinking real hard while E.J. and Nerk was working on the hole, but I didn't seem no taller, so I says to E.J., "It don't work."

"Don't work?" he says. "You ain't been at it but five minutes."

"I was believing it would only take five minutes."

"Jake, if you ain't a knucklehead, then I'm FDR." Then he put his ear to the bottom of the hole and says, "I'll be hornswaggled. I can hear a bunch of Japanese talk."

"Japanese talk?" I says. "We're supposed to be goin' to China. Sam told me Chinese and Japanese ain't got none of the same words."

"You going to believe Sam over me, Jake?"

I suspected E.J. was making up the voices, so they didn't excite me none. I was sick of that hole and I weren't going to let E.J. change the subject. "If we can do anything we dern well please just by believing it hard enough," I says, "why don't we just believe that we already won the war?"

"Don't be stupid, Jake," says E.J. "There's about a billion enemy troops that all got positive altitudes that they is gonna win."

"Then whose to say there ain't a bunch of Chinamen that got a positive altitude that we ain't gonna finish this hole?"

"We gotta have a positive altitude that they don't."

I figured there weren't no end to it. E.J. kept explaining, but

I weren't listening no more. I couldn't see where one of these positive altitudes made much difference. Seemed to me a heap better to just see things the way they is. But, of course, I ain't no expert on it.

8

The Plan

Even after Pearl Harbor, Ma kept right on baking bread and rolls and taking 'em over to the Tanakas. It was downright shameful to the family. I felt powerful bad when Pa would swear and yell at her about it, but I reckon she brought it on herself.

That night when I come home from working on the hole, Ma was pulling some biscuits out of the oven. When I seen she baked up two pans full, I knowed what she was up to. Pa was off somewhere, probably mending the chicken coop.

"Jake," Ma says, "I got a late start on these biscuits and it'll be dark out soon. I'm gonna take 'em down to the Tanakas, and it sure would be nice to have a man along to watch over me."

It might have been wartime, but a feller has still got to look after his ma. I just hoped nobody would see us.

Mrs. Tanaka answered the door. She was looking mighty sickly, but even so she lit up like a hundred candles when she seen us. She shuffled us inside before I knowed what was happening and yelled something in Japanese back at Sam's bedroom. The only part of it I could make out was "Jake." Sam come clipping into the living room like it was Christmas morning. When he seen me, he smiled just like he always used to before Pearl Harbor. I could see right off he was taking this whole thing wrong.

Ma and Mrs. Tanaka got to jabbering away, and Sam come over by me on the couch. He sat there smiling and looking embarrassed. I fingered the doily on the couch's armrest.

"You been playing a lot of basketball lately, Jake?" he asked.
"Yup."

I knocked the doily off and bent over and picked it up. I noticed on the wall was hung a picture of FDR and next to it was a little American flag that'd been made into some kind of a plaque. There was also a picture of some mountain shaped like a upside down funnel with some snow on the top of it and some Japanese writing at its base. The picture of FDR and the flag didn't fool me. I knew how the Tanakas really felt. I didn't say nothing to Sam —just stared out of the front window.

After a bit, I noticed Sam weren't smiling no more. Finally, Ma and Mrs. Tanaka finished up. Me and Ma was standing on the porch and Sam was looking down at his shoes. I could see how bad he hurt. As Mrs. Tanaka was closing the door, before I even knowed what I was doing I blurted out, "Nice talking to you, Sam."

I just caught a glimpse of his smile before the door shut. As we turned to walk down the porch steps I heard him yell from inside the house, "Thanks for coming by, Jake."

I couldn't believe what I done. We walked about halfway home without talking, until Ma says, "That was a right nice thing you said to Sam."

"Right nice thing?" I says. "It was a right nice thing for a traitor to say."

Ma only smiled and took my hand. I pulled it away.

"Jake, " she says, "you done the right thing."

"How is it right, if everybody in town says no good American would be caught dead talking to one of the enemy?"

"Everybody in town don't say it. You're just listening to the wrong voices."

"Well, then, whose voice should I listen to?"

"The same one you listened to back there on the Tanakas' porch."

I could see it was no use talking to her. John was off training to fight the enemy, and here I was telling 'em how nice it was to talk to 'em. That night in my prayers I asked God to make it so nobody would ever find out what I done.

We kept digging the hole for a couple of nights after that, until finally I says, "Hey, E.J., what we gonna do when we get to the ground water?" He didn't answer me, just asked me why I was dumb as a two by four. But it weren't long after that he said it weren't enough for him to have the most positive altitude ever if me and Nerk didn't have one, so we give up on it. There weren't much use in me guarding Potter's Pond anymore neither, being as it had froze over. We'd spy on the Tanakas' house every now and again, but that was about as exciting as gathering eggs with tweezers.

E.J. said that since war ain't never supposed to be boring, he best call MacArthur on the telephone. Next day he said MacArthur weren't exactly tickled with the job we was doing. He said E.J. was the best dern captain in the whole Rooster Creek sector, and if me and Nerk didn't start working harder we was gonna be courtmarshalled.

I suggested that maybe we could start gathering gum wrappers and cigarette packages and peel off the tinfoil and press it into balls. Mr. Larson had said once in school that FDR wanted a whole bunch of tinfoil for the war effort, and there was a prize for the person who gathered the most. As far as I could figure, FDR used it to make tanks or something.

E.J. said that kind of stuff was for kids, not soldiers, because there weren't no danger to it. Then he had an idea. "I got it," he says. "It's high time we attack the Tanakas. That'd scare every other spy in the county."

I could tell right off I didn't like that idea. "MacArthur didn't say nothing about attackin' the Tanakas," I says.

"Yeah he did, but he said being as it was top secret I weren't to tell it except in an emergency. We'll use hand grenades. I seen a news reel once where the marines was pinned down by a machine gun. One of 'em crept through the jungle and threw a hand grenade, just like this." He stuck his arm straight out and whipped it over his head as he fell forward on his stomach.

"We ain't got no hand grenades," I says.

"Eggs'll do just as well. Ain't no need to kill 'em, just skeer 'em."

"They're skeert enough," I says. "Sam's so skeert he won't go near nobody no more. Eggs ain't gonna help none."

Then Nerk pops in. "What are you, Jake, one of the enemy?"

I'd have punched his lights out right then, but E.J. jumped in front of him and says, "Traitor Jake."

I shouted back, "I ain't no traitor. I want to fight more than both of you two put together. They ain't trying to kill one of your brothers."

"Calm down, Jake," E.J. says. "Me and Nerk was just using what you call psychology. That's how you get a feller to do what at first he don't want to do. We knowed all along you weren't no traitor. You're a true blue American. Bring as many eggs as you can sneak out of your cellar on Friday night and we'll meet at nine o'clock sharp."

Well, I hadn't never heard of psychology, and I knew Nerk hadn't neither, but it worked just the same. I decided I'd be careful to keep an eye out for it in the future. Between it and positive altitudes, it didn't seem a feller had a chance.

By Thursday, E.J. had the plan all figured out. He was to come down the Alpine Road and cross through Greenwoods' yard, and Nerk and me was to sneak through the mill lane. Then we was all to meet behind the snow bluff just behind the Tanakas' house.

"We'll each have two eggs," says E.J. "First I'll sneak up around the north side of the house, being careful so as not to step on no land mine. Then I'll lie my eggs down and pick up a big rock. After I break out the front window, I'll run back and get my eggs. You two crouch down low, run past me, and start throwing eggs in the window. Then I'll get my eggs and throw 'em in. We'll make our getaway up the hill through the cemetery and back home. Won't nobody know where we come from or where we went."

It was a right fancy plan, but I didn't care for it just the same. The Tanakas hadn't bombed nobody, hadn't even called nobody a name — didn't say much of anything anymore, for that matter. I don't think Sam had said more than five words in school since Pearl Harbor. He even played alone at recess, and his ma and pa didn't hardly leave the house much anymore. Besides, Ma said Mrs. Tanaka was getting sicker by the day. I decided I weren't gonna make no attack on 'em.

During recess on Friday I says to E.J. and Nerk, "You know, attackin' the Tanakas ain't no more dangerous than gathering tinfoil. Being as we is the only troops MacArthur's got in these parts, we best spend our time searching for some real enemy soldiers instead of scaring a family that don't bother nobody."

I could see by looking into E.J.'s eyes that weren't gonna work, so I says, "How about if we postpone the attack?"

That made 'em both mad. E.J. said, "We don't need no cowards along anyways."

Then they started saying over and over loud enough for everybody in the schoolyard to hear, "Jake is a traitor. Jake is a traitor."

Some other kids started into it, too. I began to walk away, and E.J. yelled, "You're a traitor, Jake. You're aidin' and bettin' the enemy's army. MacArthur'll have your hide for this."

That day I walked home alone. Ma was churning butter. She had a way of telling right off when something was bothering me, and today weren't no different. I knew I wouldn't be able to keep from telling her everything, and I was right. I told her about E.J.'s plan to attack the Tanakas. She didn't get mad at me, just quietly said, "Something like that would be too much for that woman." Then she said she had to go use the Morgans' phone. I weren't sure what Ma was up to, but when she got back she said, "I called Uncle Walt. He'll be waiting there if those scalawags try to cause any trouble." Uncle Walt was the town sheriff.

Well, I'd really done it now. I didn't want the Tanakas to get hurt, but I didn't want to get E.J. and Nerk in trouble, neither. I'd sooner be anything than a tattletale. I ran to E.J.'s and Nerk's to tell 'em about Uncle Walt, but they was both out somewheres. I figured they had called off the attack since I said I wouldn't help, so I went home. I walked real slow — I never felt so low. I didn't even stop to see the fish on account of I didn't think he'd want to see somebody like me. I didn't care no more if the whole school knew I was a traitor; I just hoped John would never find out.

When I got to school the next day I seen both E.J. and Nerk in the schoolyard, but they acted like I weren't nothing but air. I found out from Mortimer Wilde that Uncle Walt had caught 'em both by the seat of the trousers on Tanakas' property. He told 'em if they ever tried anything like that again he'd cut off their ears, send 'em to reform school, and throw away the key.

When we come back from lunch period that day, somebody'd wrote in letters about three feet high on the blackboard, JAKE IS A TRAITOR. Miss Wrenchler got all upset and erased so hard you'd have thought it was wrote in ink.

I looked over at Sam. He had his head down on his desk. By the end of the day everybody knowed what I done, and thought I was no better than Ben and Dick Arnold, them Revolutionary War traitors. I hated Sam worse than ever. On account of him, not only was my brother on the other side of the world getting shot at, but I didn't have nobody I could call a friend no more. That night I felt like crying, so I went to my room and did. It was the first night since I could remember that I didn't think about Rip Snorgan.

9

The Gift

***

Miss Wrenchler kept on as our teacher for the next couple of weeks. I guess she didn't know much about substitute teaching, because she was every bit as nice and a good mite easier than Mrs. Amber was.

The war kept right on, but we didn't stop making Christmas decorations. By and by, gifts started to pile up under the tree at the back of the classroom. It took some painful thinking, but I finally ended up getting Sarah a tolerable good gift—a Bingo game. I had Ma wrap it up nice and perty, on account of I wanted Sarah to be excited when she saw it under the tree. I carried it to school hid under my coat, since I didn't want nobody to ask about it—things was bad enough at school as it was.

One day Sam's gift for me showed up under the tree. It was one of the littlest presents there, but I knowed I shouldn't have expected no more from one of the enemy. I'd like to have had the present Avard Embry was getting. It was bigger than a shoebox, but that weren't surprising, because Avard was the luckiest kid in our class. He got to miss two weeks of school in October, just because he had scarlet fever.

I'd just as soon Sam hadn't given me a present, but I didn't know how to go about explaining to Miss Wrenchler that I didn't want no gift from one of the enemy. She treated him just like she did everybody else. She didn't seem to know about how enemy subs could get into Potter's Pond and the enemy soldiers could take Rooster Creek just like that.

Just the same, I was excited on the day we was to open the gifts, on account of I was perty sure Sarah would like the Bingo game. Miss Wrenchler picked Sarah and Melissa May Marker to hand out the presents. Sarah headed down my row glowing like a light bulb. She set my present on my desk and with a smile about a mile wide said, "Merry Christmas, Jake."

For a minute I didn't care if I was getting the smallest gift in the class. I hadn't even dared talk to Sarah since Jake Is A Traitor was wrote on the board, and here she was saying "Merry Christmas" to me like she really meant it. I felt like the star on top of the tree.

I didn't open my gift right off, on account of I was watching Sarah. When she opened hers, she was as excited as a billygoat in the town dump. "It's a Bingo game!" she shouted. "I love it!"

Miss Wrenchler heard her and thought the game was a right fine idea. "The whole class can play it," she said. "Who gave it to you?"

"Jake," Sarah said, and then she looked over at me. I looked away real quick, but I know she saw I was looking at her. My ears was warming up, which was a sure sign that my face was gettin' redder'n a beet, but I was excited about what Miss Wrenchler had said, anyways. I thought maybe if the whole class played my game, kids would stop calling me a traitor.

I watched Sam as he opened up his gift. It'd been the last present to appear under the tree, and for a while there I was thinking that whoever had drawed his name wasn't gonna get him anything. His package was long and skinny and looked like it might be a pencil, but when he got it open I could see it was a stick with a little American flag on it. It was from Anna Mae. I guess she gave it to him as a joke. He unrolled it and then rolled it up again real quick and wrapped the paper back around it — like he didn't want nobody seeing it. I don't think anybody but me seen him open it, not even Anna Mae. Everybody else was whooping it up good, but Sam just pulled out his history book and started reading.

I was about the last one to open a gift. Mine was small, but it was perty heavy. I could tell Sam was watching me, even though he kept acting like he was reading his book. Since I didn't have no scissors, the ribbon took me a while to get off. When I pulled off the soft wrap-tissue paper, my hands started shaking. I couldn't believe it. All my life I'd wanted a Jack Armstrong Walkometer, and now here I was holding one in my hands.

I turned to look at Sam. He acted like he'd been reading the book all the time. There was a note folded up inside that I unfolded and read:

"To my best friend, Jake. I knowed you sent for one of these, but they ran out. I sent in before you did, and when mine come, I decided never to use it until you got yours. I hope you like it. Sam."

Miss Wrenchler saw what I had and she come to my desk and said, "My stars, Jake! That looks like it cost a good bit more than a dime."

"No," I says, "it only costs a dime if you send two Wheaties box tops in to Jack Armstrong."

"What is it?" she asked.

It was hard to believe that somebody got to be a teacher without knowing what a walkometer is, but I explained it to her anyways. I told her if you strapped it to your waist, it would click for every step you took, and that would tell you how far you walked. Jack Armstrong uses one of 'em wherever he goes.

For a few minutes I felt like I was living a dream. I'd felt like dying when I'd got the letter back saying my order couldn't be filled. But now I was holding a walkometer in my hand and it was mine. I clipped it to my pocket and walked around the room once. With every step it would make a sound inside like something was falling.

I was happy, but not as happy as I always thought I'd be if I ever got a walkometer. Problem was there was nobody to get excited about it with. I walked home alone as usual, but for the first time since Pearl Harbor I took the short way down Alpine Road past Sam's house. I hadn't meant to; it was just that I was so interested in how far I was walking that I weren't paying attention to where I was walking. It was just a little over a mile and a half from the school to Sam's house.

As I was checking my walkometer across the street from the Tanakas' house, I seen Sam coming down the mill lane, shuffling along, looking down at the road. He was holding the flag at his side.

I could tell by the way he was walking that he hurt awful bad inside. I knowed just how he felt. A gift weren't worth much if you didn't have nobody to share the happiness of getting it. Then it struck me that I was probably the only person in all of Rooster Creek who knowed how he felt. I wanted to stay and thank him for the walkometer and tell him that I knowed just what he was going through, but I couldn't bring myself to do it. And maybe I didn't understand what he was feeling. Everybody at school hated us both, but I didn't deserve it. Anyways, I knowed it would be downright unpatriotic to thank him for anything, and besides, things at school would get even worse for me if it got around that I had.

I felt guilty I'd felt sorry for him; on account of everybody said he was one of the enemy. I decided a walkometer didn't exactly make up for having your brother shipped off to get shot at, so I took off running toward my house. I didn't know whether Sam seen me or not, and I didn't care.

When I got home, I felt bad about how much I'd enjoyed the present. I put the walkometer in my drawer, and I weren't sure if I'd ever feel like taking it out.

10

December Rain

I didn't care much for carrots, so I always et around 'em when we had lamb stew. I'd save 'em for last on account of I'd just as soon have all the misery in one lump at the end instead of letting it spoil my whole meal. I was just starting on the carrots when Ma says, "Jake, Mrs. Tanaka's been in an awful way this past while. Why don't I pour some of this lamb stew into a pan and cover it with tinfoil. If we hurry, we can run it up to the Tanakas and it'll still be warm when they get it."

Well, that was one mistake I weren't gonna make again. Everybody at school might've thought I was a traitor, but I still had my principles. I told Ma she was gonna have to take it herself, on account of I had to go out and slop the pigs. That was John's chore before he joined the marines, and it was enough to make me want to join, too. Seemed like all I did since he'd been gone was slop them things. Fact is, the pigs could've waited and Ma knowed it. Pa knowed it, too, but he said, "Leave the boy alone, woman. Let him go about his chores."

We finished eating in silence. Ma was the first to get up from the table. She poured out the stew like she said she was gonna, wrapped her shawl around her, and walked out of the front door without saying goodbye or nothing to me and Pa. I'd always get an empty feeling inside when I did something to make my ma feel bad, but there was times when a fellow just had to do what he figured was right.

After I slopped the pigs, I shot a few baskets in the barn. One thing I like about playing ball in the winter is that you don't sweat as easy. Not that I got anything against sweating—I think it's a right manly thing to do—it's just that it was a nice change not to.

By and by, I went back to the house. Ma was back from the Tanakas and was over in Pa's rocker, rocking real slow and gazing out of the window. When I walked closer, I could see that her cheeks was glistening wet. Before I could ask her what the matter was, she said, so soft I almost didn't hear her, "She passed away."

"She what?" I asked.

"She died."

I didn't say nothing, just set my hand on the rocker handle and let it move back and forth with the chair. Finally I says, "Ma, I never thought she'd die."

When I said that, she grabbed my hand and pulled me onto her lap. She put my arm around her neck, and I didn't feel much like I wanted to move it. We was right there by the front window, and anybody that might have walked by woulda seen me there in my ma's lap like some kind of baby, but I didn't care none. I was just glad to have a ma. Then Ma said, "I don't know if she died of cancer or of a broken heart." She kept rocking real slow, and the only sound in the whole house was the creaking the rocker made on the wood floor of the kitchen.

By and by I says, "Ma, I don't care if she was Japanese, I ain't never knowed a nicer lady."

Ma kept on looking out of the window, held me a little tighter, and said, "Jake, as far as the Lord is concerned, it was just one of his precious children who died. He don't see his children as yellow, black, or white. He just sees them as his children and loves them all the same."

"Then why'd he make 'em different in the first place?" I asked. "Seemed like that causes nothing but problems."

"I don't rightly know. Maybe he did it so we could learn to see 'em like he does, made us all different colors just so we could learn how to see right past 'em — so we'd learn to look at a person's soul instead of their skin."

"E.J. says he made 'em different so we'd know they was up to no good — and he ain't the only one I heard say it."

"Do you believe that, Jake? Do you believe that about the Tanakas?"

"No, Ma, but I'm just trying to do what people says is right."

"It don't matter much what people say is right; it just matters what's right."

"Well, if you say one thing and somebody else says somethin' else, how am I supposed to know what's right?"

"Don't listen to either one of us. All we do is drowned out the most important voice. What does the voice inside you say? Listen to yourself."

I weren't sure I understood what Ma was getting at, but I do know I had a quiet feeling inside, and it was the first time I felt that way since before Pearl Harbor.

Before I knowed it, tears was running down my face. It felt like everything I'd held inside for so long was spurting out like the water out of a busted fire hydrant. Ma was crying right along with me.

"Jake," Ma said, "you ain't particular good at hating. Why don't you do what you're good at?"

I didn't answer back, just wiped my nose on my wrist and stared out of the window and gave things a good think as we rocked. By and by, I pulled her hand from around me, ran into my room, and got the walkometer out of my drawer. I'd never showed it to her before, but for some reason I wanted her to know that Sam gave it to me. She took me back into her lap, and every time she'd rock, the walkometer would click. I held her tight as she rocked back and forth.

I must have fallen asleep there in her lap, because I woke up the next morning in my bed. My walkometer was on the dresser.

As best I could figure, we must have rocked for pert near a mile before Ma put me to bed. It was raining. That was a peculiar thing in Rooster Creek for December. I figured I was always the first person in the county to know when it was raining, on account of I had a tin roof over my bedroom.

I moseyed on into the kitchen, but Ma wasn't fixing pancakes like she usually did on Saturday mornings. I looked around and seen a note on the counter that said: "Some oatmeal cereal is warming on the stove. I've gone up to Mrs. Tanaka's funeral. Be back around ten o'clock."

I walked over and took the pan off the stove without even taking the lid off the cereal. I just threw my coat on and walked out of the door. It was freezing rain, a lot colder than snow woulda been, and it weren't long before I was wishing I brought my hat, but I didn't go back for it. The rain was falling hard — felt like it was falling right through me. I could see Potter's Pond in the distance, but I didn't even look for any enemy subs.

I ran all the way to the cemetery. It was in the middle of the valley, not but a stone's throw from the Tanakas' house, on a little hill that stuck up so you could see all the way to Shepherdsville looking one way and all the way to South Fork looking the other — without even moving your feet. I always figured it was a shame to put a cemetery on the prettiest spot in the world, but once you'd put a cemetery in, there weren't no changing your mind — at least, not until the resurrection, when everybody cleared out for good.

The road only went as far as the bottom of the hill; you had to walk up the rest of the way to the graves. After I come through the mill lane, I could see that Mr. Morley's hearse was parked at the bottom of the hill and a group of people was standing around it. When I got a little closer, I seen they was Ma, Mr. Tanaka, Sam, and Mr. Morley. When Mr. Morley seen me, his eyes lit up and he hollered out, "Hurry up, Jake. One more hand ought to do it."

The heavy oak casket was sitting on two long poles that stuck out on either end. Mr. Morley grabbed one end of the pole on one side, and Ma took hold of it on the other side of the casket. Mr. Tanaka was on the other end of the pole Mr. Morley held, and me and Sam grabbed the end on the other side. Me and Sam's shoulders was touching. I didn't say nothing to him, on account of I weren't sure if it was the right time to be opening my mouth, but I tried to look at him so he'd know that I knowed how bad he felt.

I been to funerals before, but Ma was the first lady pallbearer I ever seen. Fact is, there weren't much choice about the matter. I told Sam nobody'd come because of the freezing rain, but I reckon he knew better. It took us about five minutes to get the casket up to the top of the hill. Just after we made it to the top, Miss Wrenchler come puffing up.

Mr. Morley made a real nice speech. He said some mighty perty things about Mrs. Tanaka, how even though she weren't Christian, she was always good to everybody and never did no complaining. When he finished, I said "Amen" loud enough to make sure Sam and his pa heard me. We all helped cover over the casket, because the grave diggers had said it would cost five dollars less if they didn't have to come back. It was cold and awful muddy, but nobody seemed much worried about getting dirty.

Sam and me walked down the hill together. Ma was up a few paces talking with Mr. Tanaka. I turned to Sam and says, "My ma told me your ma is an angel now and that someday you're gonna see her again. She'll ask you how you been doing and you'll give her the biggest, longest hug in history." Ma hadn't really told me the part about the hug, but I couldn't see it happening no other way.

I could see that Sam was crying. I put my arm around his shoulder and whispered, "Gomen nasai about your ma—about everything." He didn't say nothing back on account of he didn't need to. We was best friends and we both knowed it. Deep down I think we always knowed it.

After the funeral, things was awful different. I don't mean with E.J., Nerk, and the other kids at school—they still wouldn't have nothing to do with me. It was just that it didn't hurt like it used to. I had my best friend back, and I reckon one best friend is better than all the rest put together.

Me and Sam decided we was gonna collect enough tinfoil to build twenty tanks, and everywhere we went we took the walkometer. I'd wear it a mile and Sam'd wear it a mile. Gathering tinfoil woulda been hard work, but we always had plenty to talk about, and talking makes work considerable easier. Anyways, it beat digging holes to China by a long shot.

We searched everywhere, even rummaged through every inch of the town dump. That weren't exactly the most pleasantest job around, but the dump was chuck full of tinfoil. We'd spend a lot of time behind the stores, too. There was some amazing things back there, and the smell was about halfway between a grocery store and the town dump. We'd bring back what we found every day and roll it into balls. We kept 'em in Sam's front room. By the end of January, our first ball was the size of a baseball. After that we started on another ball. Come the first of April, we had five baseballs of tinfoil, and if that don't seem like much to you, maybe you best try it sometime.

We might have got more, except we always had to be on the lookout for Rip Snorgan. He chased us a couple of times at night, but we outran him every time. We never did get a good look at him, on account of he was as sly as a fox. But we heard him breathing, and we could hear his footsteps as he chased us.

At first Sam and Mr. Tanaka had a hard time getting by, but Ma'd fix up supper for them every night. I'd stay and eat with 'em now and again, on account of Ma always packed a good mite more food than they could eat. I'd eat again when I got home. I reckon I ain't never had it so good.

I didn't care much anymore what E.J. and them thought about me and Sam. They didn't have much to do with us, for the most part. The only thing that kept picking away at my insides was thinking about what John would think when he found out me and Sam was friends. I knowed if I could sit down and explain things he'd understand, but I weren't too good at writing letters.

We got word back one day just before school was to let out that John ran through a whole slew of machine-gun bullets to rescue some feller, and he got some kind of medal for it. A couple of days later there was a story all about it in the Rooster Creek *Gazette*. John was drawed so as to look like Dick Tracy in a soldier's uniform, and the picture showed him pulling another GI back into a bunker. I was awful excited about things until I read in the article next to the picture that John got shot and was coming home. Ma and Pa hadn't told me nothing about him getting shot. I ran crying all the way home.

Before I could say anything, Ma hugged me and said he only got shot in the arm, and that after a while it would be good as new. When I heard that, I perked up in a hurry. It was a week before John made it home. Me and Sam kept right on collecting tinfoil, and that took my mind off waiting some, but just the same it was the longest week of my life.

11

The Parade

John could only hug me with one arm, on account of the other was in a sling. Still, it was the best hug I ever had. The first thing he said to me was, "I understand I'm not the only war hero in this family."

"How's that?" I says.

"Ma wrote me that you and Sam Tanaka have gathered more tinfoil for the war effort than any other ten kids in this county."

I weren't sure John understood everything, and I figured this would be as good a time as any to explain. "You sure you remember Sam, John?"

"Of course I do. He's the little Japanese kid who used to shoot baskets in our barn. He wrote me a letter just after I left telling me how proud you was of me. You sure are lucky to have a friend like that, Jake."

I couldn't believe what I was hearing. I felt like a double-yoked egg for all the worrying I done, but it didn't matter much now. I smiled so wide that John started laughing. "Jake," he said, "I understand this old town is gonna have a parade for me. If I'm a hero, then you and Sam are, too. We've all been working for the same cause. I don't think it would be fair unless you and your friend Sam rode in the parade with me. I'll pick you up in school tomorrow at ten-thirty sharp."

That night I thanked the Lord in my prayer for the best brother and the best friend a feller ever had. I should have prayed that I'd be able to go to sleep; it felt like the night before Christmas.

Sometimes you can just about feel people's eyes looking at you. That's how it was when John asked Miss Wrenchler to let me and Sam leave with him for the parade. I guess more people was looking at Sam than was looking at me. They'd have easier believed Sam was the Pope come down from the Vatercan than an honest-to-goodness hero, but there was John treating him like he was MacArthur hisself. And if that weren't enough, John jerks up straight and whips off the smartest salute you ever did see aimed right at me and Sam and says, "We best hurry, men, or we'll be late for the big parade."

The three of us marched out into the hall and John put his good arm around both me and Sam. That's how we walked till we got to the stairs. We was a team to beat anything.

We come out of the side door of the school and woulda cut across the lawn, but since heroes ain't the kind to go around breaking school rules, we stayed smack in the middle of the sidewalk. As we walked along, I took a gander about and it seemed to me the grass was greener and the sky bluer than I ever seen 'em before. Leaves was sprouting on the trees, and bees was sitting on most every yellow dandelion. Why, throw in a native or two and you could've easy mistook old Rooster Creek for one of them perty places in E.J.'s ma's *National Geographics*. I was feeling about as good inside as things was looking outside.

We got to the main sidewalk, and I about fell over when I seen three army jeeps lined up in front of the fire station. I seen plenty of jeeps before, but never outside of a news reel, and I loved 'em better than any other kind of car or truck, or whatever in turnation they are. E.J. used to tell us MacArthur was fixing to send us a jeep and a tank, but we never seen hide nor hair of neither.

As we walked past the jeeps, John says, "We'll be riding in one of them babies in the big parade." I was so excited you'd have thought somebody'd just told me the school burnt down. My heart was beating so fast I was afraid I'd crack a rib.

About that time Mayor Beck comes trotting out of the fire station. Soon John and the mayor was shaking hands so hard the mayor's cheeks wobbled around like a couple of pig bladders. A few seconds longer and I believe they might have broke his nose.

"We sure are proud of you, John," he says. Then he looked around smiling and said it again. The mayor had a mighty peculiar habit of saying everything twice. I guess he figured folks would think he knew twice as much. Then he grabbed John and hauled him over to a bunch of fellers dressed in army uniforms.

"General," he says, "this is Rooster Creek's own hometown hero, John Denning."

He started to say that again, too, but the general he jumps in, grabs John's hand, and says, "Private Denning, it's a great honor to meet a marine whose bravery has inspired us all."

Then the mayor grabbed John away again and hustled him over to a bunch of fellers with big purple badges that had Parade Official wrote on 'em. John started talking, but the mayor was frowning and shaking his head so hard you'd have thought his sister was asking his permission to marry a Republican. Then John says loud enough for me and Sam to hear, "No, I want 'em both right in the jeep with me."

The mayor stopped shaking his head, but before his cheeks could stop shaking, the general put his arm around John's shoulders and says, "Private Denning, what a hero wants, a hero gets."

The next thing I know, John shouts over at Sam and me, "Boys, come on over here. The general wants to meet two more heroes."

I don't mind telling you, I was skeert. I'd never met a army latrine digger, let alone a real general. We walked over and the general says, "I understand you boys collected more tinfoil than anybody else in your school."

By this time I was too nervous to spit, much less talk to a general, but Sam was smiling and he says all official-like, "Yes, sir."

Then the general smiles and says, "We want you two heroes to ride on each side of Private Denning, so jump in this back seat and I'll sit up by the driver. We'll have ourselves the biggest parade this old town has ever seen."

We was up there in a flash. It was awful squashed in that back seat, but it felt good to have my arm pushing up against John's. I felt like the closer I could get to him, the more of a hero I was. Then Sam looks over at me and shouts, "Hey, Jake, don't this beat all?"

I looked over back at him and says, "What a hero wants, a hero gets."

John put his good arm around me and pulled me even closer. "How are you two heroes doing?" he asked. We didn't say nothing back, just kind of smiled and stuck our chests out.

About that time the high school band comes driving up in a big yeller bus that had Kilroy Was Here wrote in black paint on the side. As the band members jumped out in their red uniforms, a lot of 'em was straining their necks so as to get a better look at John. Some of the older girls was squealing like they was looking at Clark Gable hisself, but them squeals was all for my big brother. One of 'em shouted "Hubba hubba," but when John looked at her she turned red as her uniform.

After they was all out of the bus, K. J. Bird, the band leader, blowed a whistle and all of a sudden everybody was standing in perfect rows and there weren't nobody squealing, nor hardly even breathing. Then out of all them shiny horns comes a bunch of music that made my back feel like it was turning to orange jello. They started marching but didn't go nowhere — like a band can do — and our jeep driver backed out onto Center Street and drove right up behind 'em and stopped.

Mayor Beck hollered out from the jeep behind ours, "General, it's ten minutes to twelve. We ought to wait here until noon."

The general muttered something about the mayor being too big for his breeches telling a general what to do — but he smiled as he turned around and said, "Yeah, we'll wait. We don't want anybody in town to miss the parade. Nothing better than a hometown hero for war bond sales."

People was coming from every direction. There was easy a million of 'em, maybe two, and I'll bet they'd come from as far away as South Fork. As they went by they'd shout things like, "Go get 'em, John," "You sure have made us proud," and "You put Rooster Creek on the map."

While we was waiting, a real nice lady come over and said, "Private Denning."

"Yes, ma'am," says John. "What can I do for you?"

"Well," she says, "It's just that my boy is in the Pacific now. He's such a good boy, and seeing you makes me homesick to see him. He went into the navy the same day you joined the marines."

"Maybe I know him," says John. "What's his name?"

"Rip," she replied. "Rip Snorgan."

Me and Sam about fell out of the jeep.

"Sure I know him, ma'am," says John. "You be sure and give him my best the next time you write to him."

I'll tell you one thing. I was dern glad I hadn't told John about the times I ran myself silly thinking Rip was on my trail. I'd have come across as a grade A fool.

Come twelve o'clock, the mayor stood up in his jeep, stuck his hand straight up in the air, and whipped it down. He was doing his derndest to look dignified, but when the jeep driver started up a bit too fast he lost his balance, fell down onto the back of the jeep, and slid off onto the road.

He didn't hurt hisself, on account of he landed on a portion of his body with plenty of padding to spare, but he was hopping mad just the same. Matter of fact, he said a few words to the jeep driver that I ain't never heard nobody say, let alone a mayor, and he said 'em more than twice, too.

Anyways, by now K. J. Bird had the band playing one of the most powerful nice songs anybody ever wrote. I don't know what the name of it was, but it had me sitting up straighter than a fence post. I couldn't believe this was all happening to me. There I was next to the greatest, bravest war hero of all times, and there was my best friend, Sam, right there in the jeep with me. And in the front seat was sitting a real live, honest-to-goodness army general.

We turned the corner by Chipman's Store and started down Main Street. People was sitting and standing all over the sidewalk, and some was even on top of the stores. I never seen the town so excited, not even when John and the rest of the basketball team rode the fire engine through town after they won the state championship. Both the grade school and the high school had let out by now for the parade.

People was cheering and waving their arms. It was so noisy with the band playing and all the shouting that I couldn't tell everything people was saying, but I heard somebody yell, "Hey, Jake." I turned around, and I'll be derned if it weren't Sarah. I waved right at her and she looked up at her ma, proud enough to burst.

People was shouting, "John, we're proud of you."

I could even hear some saying, "Lookin' good, Sam." Sam was smiling that smile of his and waving like he had a bee up his sleeve.

We passed People's State Bank and headed for Gamble's Hardware. After that we went by Dixon Taylor Russell's furniture store and then Cook's Ice Cream. Mr. Cook was there in his white cap, his white shirt, and his white pants. He was shouting at the top of his voice, "Come back after, John, and I'll make you a malt. You two boys come along, too."

That was just about the nicest thing I heard in the whole parade, on account of I like malts at Cook's Ice Cream better than I like any food that's ever been discovered. There weren't no question about it, this was the happiest day of my life.

All during the parade I kept a sharp eye out for E.J. I weren't sure he'd come, on account of I knowed how bad he hated Sam and me, and I knowed if he did come he'd be awful jealous. He weren't too partial to anybody having no importance except himself.

By now we was just about to the church, which is where we was going to turn so as to end up in Rooster Creek Park for the speeches. There was more people on the north side of the park than there had been anywhere on the sidewalk in front of the stores.

Then I seen E.J. over by the old rock drinking fountain. He seen me see him, and he looked the other way. "There's E.J.," I shouted at Sam.

"Where, where?"

"Right there. The side of the fountain."

"You mean E. J. Courtner?" John asked.

"Yeah."

By this time the band was moving over onto the grass of the park, and our jeep was waiting to pull forward to park.

John shouted, "E.J., E.J.!" His voice boomed across the street like a cannon. I never seen E.J. so skeert, not even when I flipped that cobra on his shoulder. He looked like he wanted to run away, but he was too skeert to do even that. John yelled, "Come here!"

E.J. still didn't move, so I shouted, "Come here, E.J., he ain't gonna hurt you!"

E.J. walked over like a dog ready for a whipping, but when John stuck out his hand and says, "Shake hands, E.J., old buddy," E.J. smiled so hard half his gums was showing. I never seen nobody as proud as E.J. when he shook hands with a real hero.

The jeep moved forward, but E.J. he just kept right on standing there. Then he started shouting, "Nerk, Nerk, did you see that? Did you see that? I shook hands with a hero, a real hero. Nerk, I'll bet MacArthur told him all about me."

Then E.J. ran back closer to the jeep and yells, "Jake, Sam, I'll see ya after." After that he turned to some people from South Fork or somewheres and told 'em, "Jake and Sam are my friends. I know 'em personally." People was looking at E.J. like he was a hero, too, and I don't believe he was minding it one ioter.

After everybody settled in the park, the program started. First the mayor gave a talk which weren't too exciting the first time, nor the second neither. Then the general he stands up and says that if we are gonna win the war we best buy a whole ton of war bonds and be as brave as Private John Denning. When he said that, people started yelling and cheering.

After that John stood up to give a speech. "I ain't really a hero," he says. "The real heroes are people like Kent Amber, who have given their lives for freedom."

Then he asked Mrs. Amber to come up. I hadn't seen her since Pearl Harbor. She was awful skinny and walked slower than she used to. She was crying hard, and John puts his arm around her and says, "She has given a son for her country. No one can give more."

When John said that, there weren't nobody that cheered. It was so quiet I could hear the oak leaves rustling. John was having a hard time talking. As best I understand it, heroes ain't supposed to cry, but it sure seemed like John was close to doing just that. I know I was.

John thanked Mrs. Amber for coming up. When she started to go down the steps to her seat in front of the bandstand, everybody stood up and cheered and clapped for what seemed like a ternity.

Then John says, "It's times like this when we all wish there weren't any wars, when we wish everybody could be friends — friends like my little brother and his friend, Sam. Come up here, Jake and Sam."

I was powerful surprised, and I know ol' Sam was, too. I stood there on the stage feeling kind of funny at first, but then everybody started clapping and shouting and whistling. I looked at Sam and he was smiling a world's record smile. I felt all tingly inside and I think I was smiling even bigger than Sam.

E.J. had pushed his way to the front, and him and Nerk was sitting on the corner of the bandstand right in front of Uncle Walt. Uncle Walt normally weren't the pleasantest feller around, and any other time he'd have had E.J. and Nerk off that bandstand in about a millionth of a second, but today he didn't lift a finger.

As the cheering started to die down, somebody yelled from the back of the crowd, "Get that Sam kid off the stage. He ain't no hero."

It was dead quiet for a second or two, but then everybody commenced cheering all over again for me and Sam. There was some kind of scuffle back where the voice come from. Uncle Walt jumped up and started making his way back there as fast as he could.

Sam was smiling like he hadn't heard nothing. I heard, but I didn't bother listening on account of I was listening to another voice.